I0526437

MEMOIRS OF A
HUSTLER

First Edition

Published by The Nazca Plains Corporation
Las Vegas, Nevada
2010

ISBN: 978-1-935509-96-7

Published by

The Nazca Plains Corporation ®
4640 Paradise Rd, Suite 141
Las Vegas NV 89109-8000

PUBLISHER'S NOTE
MEMOIRS OF A HUSTLER is a work of fiction created wholly
by *Lew Bull'*s imagination. All characters are fictional and any
resemblance to any persons living or deceased is purely by accident.
No portion of this book reflects any real person or events.

Cover,
Alexey Utemov and Les Byerley

Art Director,
Blake Stephens

DEDICATION

To all the boys and young men who have
hustled to bring happiness to others.

MEMOIRS OF A
HUSTLER

First Edition

Lew Bull

CONTENTS

CHAPTER 1

I stood naked at the window of the darkened room, looking out. The only light that lit up my silhouetted body was from the glow of the street lights five floors below. There was almost silence, except for the gentle rain that pattered against the windowpane and the occasional sound of a car traveling along the wet street. I felt a warm hand rest on my naked butt and teasingly begin to explore its shape. The hand slid over the smooth round flesh, caressing it.

"Why don't you come to bed," whispered the voice in my ear. "It's warmer there."

I turned and in the dim light from the street, I saw the smiling face of Marc behind me. I smiled back.

"Why are you standing here?" asked Marc, wrapping his arm around my slim waist.

"I was just looking out of the window."

Marc moved to my side and peered out of the rain-spattered window, and then let his gaze go down to the street level.

"Were you watching them?" he asked referring to the few young men who hovered around the street below, seeking shelter.

I followed his gaze to the street and saw five or six young men, some trying to stay out of the rain in a bus shelter, while others positioned themselves in the sheltered entrances to shops. It was 2 a.m. on a weekday.

"I'm so glad that you're not down there, Chad," said Marc, squeezing me closer to him. "Come on, come back to bed."

We made our way back to the warmth of his bed, where we cuddled closer and Marc began kissing me while his warm hands explored my slim body.

I liked Marc. He had been one of my regulars and I must admit he was one of the few men that I had had feelings for.

"You know, I always had feelings for you, Marc."

"I know. I felt it every time we were together, and I know you still have those feelings, just as I have them for you, but what's happening down there is past, so forget it and go to sleep."

Marc cradled my head to his chest and I smelt the fresh soapy smell of his naked body. I was glad that I had someone dear to me in my life and I knew that I had made Marc happy by being a part of his life.

But, things never used to be like this. Things were very different three years ago, before I met Marc and before he took me into his life and cared for me.

CHAPTER 2

THE BEGINNING

I had just celebrated my nineteenth birthday and had left high school, but didn't know what to do with my life. Many of my friends had chosen to go to college but I'd never had the urge to go, maybe because I found studying a rather daunting task. I wasn't one of those natural academics, so any opportunity to get out of studying would make my day for me.

All my short life, my parents had basically said I could do as I pleased, but that didn't mean that they had washed their hands of me. Au contraire! My mother sat me down and spoke to me; then my father sat me down and spoke to me; and not to be outdone, my grandmother on my dad's side sat me down and spoke to me. My mother asked what I wanted to become and I said a sports star. My father asked me what I wanted to become and I said an accountant. My grandmother asked me what I wanted to become and I said a stripper. Naturally, when the three of them got together to compare notes, there was total confusion, but little did they realize just how right I was. The career I had chosen combined all three aspects, if they had thought about it. I became a hustler!

If you consider this occupation, you'll see how being a sports star, an accountant and a stripper all come into it. The sports star aspect meant that I would keep myself fit and in shape; after all I wanted people to desire my body and looks. The accounting aspect was how I made my money and kept it. As for the stripper! Well that's self explanatory – my clothes were constantly coming off.

My parents and grandmother all thought I was having them on when I said I was going to become a hustler, but they soon realized that I had been serious. Of course, I must add that I did get some support in choosing this career from another source.

I had been asked to be a DJ at a friend's birthday party and as the evening progressed and the drinks flowed, I went from being a DJ to entertaining. Now you might wonder what sort of entertaining, well let me tell you. The host of the party said that the party needed livening up and would I do something about the music. Well, there was very little I could about the music that I had at my disposal, so I opted for the next best thing: a strip show.

I decided to take a chance and see what the reaction would be. After all, most of the guests had already consumed a fair amount of alcohol, so doing a strip show might not bring shame to the family hosting the party. I selected a piece of music, *Big Spender* from the show *Sweet Charity,* and that will give you some idea of the selection of music we had at our disposal – no wonder the party was drooping. I turned up the volume, headed onto the make-shift dance floor and began my show. I danced, writhed wriggled my ass and then I began to take off my shirt. Now I must say, I have always prided my body; not that I spent every day at the gym, but when I had the opportunity, I did manage to work out and I played sport, so that helped a little. Once my shirt went flying off, there were squeals of delight from the women and a few drunken guys. The next to go flying in different directions were my shoes, which I never managed to find after the show, and soon my jeans followed. As seductively as I could make it, I unzipped my fly, wriggled my ass again, turned my back to my audience and began to push my jeans down towards my ankles. At the sight of my white briefs, the cheers and hoots increased. I tried to step out of my jeans, but found the task difficult. After much stumbling and almost falling over, I managed to skip out of them and danced around the room with my package bouncing in my briefs. The funny thing was that, although the crowd was enjoying my pantomime display, I found myself becoming aroused by the fact that I was half naked in front of a crowd of people and was enjoying myself. As I danced, my mind raced through what I had done. Was I about to drop my briefs, or was I going to keep them on and end the dance?

I suppose the decision to reveal all or not, was taken out of my hands, when David, a school friend of mine rushed forward, grabbed hold of the waistband of my briefs and shucked them to the ground. In the turmoil, I stumbled and fell to the floor and David ran off with my briefs, ripped. I lay there laughing hysterically until I realized that I was bare to the entire party; my semi-erection for all to see.

That was the start of my career. I had received money for doing something out of the ordinary. Well, being a DJ is not out of the ordinary, but shedding one's clothes in public is; and I enjoyed it.

Obviously I was still staying at home with my parents so it was difficult to fulfill my career as a stripper as every time I said I had an invitation to a party as a DJ, both parents and grandmother looked at me with unusual glances. They remembered what had happened the night I stripped at the party – news travels fast and although my dad thought it was a joke and laughed, my mother was not impressed. As for my grandmother, she merely scoffed the idea of men taking off their clothes in public.

"Your grandfather would be turning in his grave if he saw you doing things like that," said my grandmother when she had been told of my escapade.

For all I knew, my grandfather was turning in his grave because he hadn't had the opportunity to do what I'd done, but I never told my grandmother that.

"Why don't you come and watch, Gran?" I tried to say, but she just scoffed at the idea again.

"I couldn't think of anything worse than looking at someone's dangly bits flopping all over the place," she sternly reprimanded.

At least I knew where each of my family stood on the subject of stripping, but this was not going to deter me as the money was good.

I received a few invitations to strip at parties and on one occasion, I was approached by someone to perform at a bachelor party.

"Are you sure you don't mean it's a party for the bride and her friends?" I enquired.

"No, it's a guy's party and we want you to strip for the bridegroom."

I thought this rather odd, but what the hell, money is money, so I agreed. The date and time was given and instructions were clearly made on what I could and could not do.

"Can you do a theme strip?" asked the man, inviting me.

"Like what?"

"Well, you know; something unusual."

I still didn't know what he had in mind.

"Can you be a little more specific?" I asked.

"You know something in leather or dress like a cowboy; that sort of thing."

"Sure, I can do that."

I went home and thought about what outfit to wear, but I wasn't the sort of person who had a wardrobe filled with outrageous costumes, so I turned to my mother.

"What did you have in mind, Chad?"

"I don't know, Mum, but whatever I decide on, I'll have to borrow it from somewhere."

"Go to the costume hire shop and see what they've got," suggested my mother.

Thank goodness for mothers. They always seem to come up with clever ideas. I made my way to the costume hire shop and found an outfit for the night.

I duly arrived at the venue early so that I could get changed, but above all, I wanted to see if it actually was a party of men. Sure enough, when all the guests had arrived, there wasn't a female in sight. The guy who booked me found me in the toilet, as this was to be my change room, and I asked why they wanted a male stripper instead of a female one.

"It's a bit awkward," he answered, not really wanting to volunteer a reason.

"In what way?"

"Well, you see the groom's gay."

I was shocked by this revelation.

"But why's he getting married if he's gay?"

"Because the girl's pregnant and he's prepared to marry her so the child has a father," was the answer.

"Is it his child?"

"Heavens no! He likes the girl and it's obviously a marriage of convenience, that's all."

Who was I to criticize someone else's feelings about another human being? The fact that the baby would have a father was a noble idea, but I just wondered what their future would be like.

The guy who booked me, whose name was Fred, handed me the agreed amount of money and I stuffed it into my jeans' pocket.

"Will I see you at the end of the show?" I asked Fred.

"I'll pop by to thank you," he replied and left me to change into my costume.

I began to strip and climb into my costume for the show, but while I did this, the toilet was constantly being visited by various men who watched with interest as I dressed. I wasn't sure whether they actually needed the toilet or if they were just curious to see a half naked man in the toilet.

At last, the time arrived for me to do my show. I walked out of the toilet, where I'd been all night and went into the lounge are of this bar-like venue and waited for my cue. Fred had pointed out the groom to me so I at least knew who to perform to.

My chosen music started and I raced out into the lounge and started dancing. I was dressed as a Red Indian Chief with flowing feathered headdress, bare chest with streaks of 'war paint' over it, a black Speedo under my mini feathered 'skirt' and a pair of moccasins on my feet.

I stomped my feet a la war dance, whooped it up and wriggled my ass for the men. When I first appeared on the impromptu stage, which was actually just the lounge floor, I received whoops of cheers as I don't think they realized a guy would be dancing for them. I spotted where the groom was seated and headed in his direction. He was a tall, slim man of about twenty- seven or eight, with dark cascading straight hair and deep blue eyes. His smile was broad and friendly when he saw me near him and I knew that he was happy with the fact that it wasn't a female stripper. I wriggled my ass in front of him and then decided to stand astride his legs as he sat. I started to unbutton his shirt to whistles and cheers from his friends, and then I lowered my ass onto his lap and ground it on his crotch. I was sure that I could feel him getting hard, but maybe I was wrong. He held onto my waist as I did this and all the time, he laughed and enjoyed the attention. I then leapt up and headed to the center of the room where I detached the headdress and flung it in the direction of Fred, who I hoped would look after my props. I then danced among the other men, feeling their hands rub across my chest and waist. The occasional hand also landed on my ass, which I didn't mind at all; then very casually, I slowed down the tempo and began to seductively slide my Speedo down at the back, allowing them to see the top of my ass crack. There were roars of cheers and more whistles until I pulled the waistband back up, covering my ass again. Then I turned my back to them and pulled my Speedo down and stepped out of it, but making sure that my hands covered my balls and cock. I continued dancing like this for a while until I knew the music was coming to an end and as the last notes of the music sounded, I released my grip on my balls and cock and turned to face the men, but at this time I'd developed a bit of a hard-on.

At the sight of my hard-on, there was an outburst of clapping and cheering and I caught sight of the groom smiling very broadly in my direction, before I fled back to the toilet to get dressed.

"Wow, that was great, Chad," said Fred, bringing my feather headdress and 'skirt' back to me.

I was standing with a towel wrapped around my waist and I thanked him for the opportunity to perform for them.

"The groom wants to come and thank you as well," said Fred, standing and admiring my body as though it was the first time he'd seen it.

Just then the groom entered.

"Well, I'll leave you two to talk," said Fred and left the toilet area.

The groom crossed to me and took me in his arms, giving me his version of a bear hug. My towel suddenly dropped to the floor and I stood naked in the arms of the man about to get married.

"Thank you, thank you. That was great fun," he said.

"You're welcome," was all I could think of to say.

He then released me and before I had a chance to bend and pick my towel, I felt his hand grab my balls and cock and squeeze them.

"You're quite a big boy, aren't you?"

I had never consciously thought of myself being 'big', but instinctively I looked down at my cock in his hands and realized that I suppose I was well hung, possibly in comparison to other nineteen year old guys.

Still holding onto me, the groom said, "How would you like to come back to my place?"

I was completely stunned as I knew that the following day he was to get married, whether for convenience or not, he was still marrying a woman. I hesitated and didn't know how to respond. I felt his hand go tighter on my cock and knew that I was beginning to get hard. He smiled at me and we merely stood and looked at each other.

"I don't even know your name," I whimpered, stupidly.

"It's Greg, but that still doesn't answer my question."

"Well Greg, I think you're very nice and all that, but I'm not sure I should be doing that with you, considering you're to get married."

"Chad; it is Chad, isn't it?"

"Yes."

"Well Chad, although I'm getting married, the agreement between my future wife and me is that there's no sex between us. I'm not into women and I'm only doing it for the baby. So what do you say?"

Again I hesitated.

"I'm extremely flattered by the offer, Greg, but …"

"…I'll pay you," said Greg cutting in.

The word 'pay' flashed through my head like a neon light flashing. I had never been propositioned like this before. Someone was actually offering to pay me to have sex with them. I became confused, but before I had a chance to think too long, Greg made my mind up for me.

"$100, take it or leave it," he said.

Another neon sign started flashing. One hundred dollars was a great deal of money to me and to turn that sort of money down was, in my mind, sacrilegious.

"I take it from the smile on your face, the answer is yes?" asked Greg.

I merely nodded.

"Well then, let's go," he added, picking up my feather headdress for me and heading out of the toilet with me following.

That was how it all started!

Back at Greg's apartment, we didn't even manage to make it to the bedroom as he pounced on me and stripped me in the lounge of his place and there on the carpet I experienced my first paid sex. As I slipped my hard cock in and out of his ass, all I saw before me were dollar signs. What was so wrong with this, I wondered. I enjoyed sex and to get paid for it was a bonus.

I could hear and see that Greg was enjoying every moment of my attacking his ass and when I came, he wanted me to stay imbedded in him and fuck him all over again; for that I never got another $100.

When we had both exhausted ourselves and lay spent on the lounge floor, Greg asked if I could visit him again once he got married because he had enjoyed my sex with him so much. I think he'd already forgotten that there would be someone else in his apartment after the following day.

"That might be awkward, Greg, as your wife will be here."

"Oh, I forgot. Well if she goes out at all and I need you, can I call you?"

If Greg was going to be happy to pay for having sex with me, I would be only too happy to accommodate him.

"Sure. Have you got a pen and paper and I'll give you my number," I replied.

Greg duly found both pen and paper and I wrote down my contact details.

"Unfortunately I can't invite you back to my place because I stay with my parents," I said rather embarrassedly.

"That's not a problem at all."

Once we had got dressed, Greg was gentlemanly enough to offer to take me back to my place, but as we neared our house, I told him to stop and I'd get out. I didn't want him to see where I lived, not because we had a crumby house, but I didn't want him pitching up unannounced and then I'd have to try and explain to my folks.

Two weeks later, I received a call from Greg.

"Hi Chad, how are things? It's Greg from the bachelor party."

"Oh hi Greg. How was the honeymoon?"

"Not very exciting. We just moseyed around, but I missed you."

He missed me! That sounded very odd for a guy who had just chosen to get married, even if he was gay. Obviously I didn't know what to say, so I kept quiet.

"Are you there?"

"Oh, yes," I replied.

"I was wondering if you weren't too busy if you'd like to come round to my place tonight. Cathy's gone to her parents and won't be back until tomorrow. You could stay the night if you'd like."

There was a hush on the line. I didn't respond as I thought of the potential plan.

"I'll pay you double to stay the night," suggested Greg.

That would mean $200 if I slept over. The temptation was great and what better deal could I ask for: I liked sex and money. I also realized that by doing this, I was becoming a slut – but that would be in the eyes of only some people! On the other hand, it could be perceived as just a business transaction. I liked the latter.

"Sure, that sounds like fun. Can I meet you somewhere?"

"I'll come and pick you up, if you'd like."

"No, no. It's OK; I'll get a cab to your place. What time do you want me round there?"

"How about six or six-thirty tonight," volunteered Greg

"Then I'll see you that your place," I replied, replacing the telephone.

"Who was that?" enquired my grandmother, when I had replaced the handset.

"Just a friend, Gran."

"No another party, I hope?"

"No, not this time, Gran. I'm going for a sleepover."

Granny's eyes took on a strange look and a furrow appeared on her brow.

"What are you thinking, Gran?"

"I've heard about sleepovers, Chad…"

"It's OK Gran; it's not with a whole group of girls."

The furrow disappeared and her eyes widened.

"You mean boys?"

"No Gran, it's just an old high school friend," I said, hoping the interrogation would end.

She merely shrugged her shoulders and waddled off to the kitchen, no doubt to inform my mother.

I went to my room, grabbed a small backpack and stuffed a few clothes into it for the morning and then waited for the clock to tick by until I could call a cab.

My mother had been rightly informed by my Gran so didn't interrogate me as much as my grandmother had. When the cab pulled up outside, she just told me to take care of myself and she'd see me the following day.

By the time I reached Greg's apartment and rung the doorbell, he had prepared dinner for us both but when I saw the table set for dinner, I noticed there were place settings for three.

"Are you expecting others?" I asked casually, indicating the third place setting.

"Yes," replied a delighted Greg, "Fred's coming round. You remember him don't you? He was my best man at the wedding."

Now I wasn't sure what was happening, but at least I knew that I'd been booked for the night and for $200, so I pushed the third person out of my mind.

By half past six, Fred had arrived and the three of us were happily seated in Greg's lounge enjoying drinks.

I must just tell you that when I saw Greg and Fred together, I wondered if they'd not had some sort of relationship at some stage. They were definitely very close friends, but how close really was none of my business.

The meal was tasty and the drinks were plentiful and as the evening progressed, so the three of us became more and more relaxed until Greg gave a yawn and suggested that he was getting tired and that bed was calling. I wasn't sure whether this was a message for Fred to leave, but if it was, he never got it.

"Well guys, I'm off to bed," said Greg, rising and heading in the direction of his bedroom.

Fred smiled at me when Greg had left and said, "Shall we join him?"

I was somewhat surprised but not worried. You see, Fred was about a year or two older than Greg and was clearly the manlier of the two. It had crossed my mind that if they'd been very close friends and there had been sex between them, I was sure that it would have been Fred to get to taste the pleasures of Greg's ass and not the other way around.

Fred rose from the seat he was in and began peeling off his clothes, so I did much the same and together we made our naked way to Greg's bedroom where we found his sitting up in bed waiting for us.

"What took you two so long?" he asked, patting the covers of the bed.

Fred pushed me towards the bed, indicating that I should climb in next to Greg then he followed me so that I was sandwiched between the two of them. The moment the covers were over us, hands were feeling everywhere, until it became so busy in the bed, that the covers were flung off and the three naked bodies had easier access to one another.

Mouths, tongues cocks and asses went in all directions and partners were constantly being swapped. First both Fred and Greg attacked my cock, both licking my thick shaft together and then as Greg continued taking my cock down his throat, so Fred attacked my ass with his probing tongue. Once Greg had lathered my cock sufficiently to his liking, he flipped over onto his side and pushed his ass up against my throbbing cock. I never had to do a thing, because Greg's hands guided my shaft deep into his waiting chute where he proceeded to clamp tightly around my shaft and start thrusting back onto my length. At the same time, I felt the stubby prodding of Fred's cock trying to break into my puckered asshole. I waited a moment and then felt Fred's cock sink slowly into me. As he pushed further, so I gasped realizing how big he was but the feeling of pleasure far outweighed any pain or discomfort that I might have been experiencing. Soon, with the thereof us tightly plugged to one another, a steady rhythm was established and our breathing and moans came in waves as each one satisfied the other.

When we tired of being in the same position, Greg turned onto his back and raised his legs for me to re-enter his warm, comforting ass and at the same time, Fred plowed straight back into me, now having become accustomed to his size. This continued until all three of us had shot our loads and collapsed exhausted in the bed, only to start up a little later. All night we changed positions, but I never got to taste Fred's ass with my cock, but that didn't worry me as I was being well and truly satisfied.

I woke in the early hours of the morning to find Greg in bed, but no Fred. I quietly rose and padded my way through to the bathroom and then into the lounge, but found no sign of Fred. When I returned to the bedroom, Greg was sitting up in bed looking very sleepy.

"Mornin," I said, slipping back into bed next to him.

"Hi there. Has Fred gone?"

"Well, I don't see him, so I assume he has."

"Never mind, maybe just the two of us can have a good time together."

I couldn't believe that this man had not had enough sex for one night, but an even bigger surprise awaited me. After I'd satisfied Greg again, we rose and made our way through to the kitchen where Greg picked up and enveloped addressed to me.

"I think this is from Fred," said Greg, handing me the envelope, "and this is from me," he added, handing me another envelope.

I opened Greg's and found two $100 bills and when I opened Fred's I found the same. I couldn't believe my luck; $400 for a night's pleasure! Now I knew that I wasn't a slut but an up and coming hustler.

CHAPTER 3

BUSINESS BEGINS

When I arrived back from Greg's apartment, my mother asked if I'd enjoyed my evening, to which I merely nodded. I couldn't tell her of my 'business' transactions, not because I was embarrassed, but you know what mothers are often like! They fire a barrage of questions until they get the answers they want.

Within the next few weeks, I found myself being 'invited' to a number of guy's places, most of them the men who had attended Greg's wedding. It's amazing the power of word-of-mouth advertising. Gradually, I found myself building up a small bank balance from my stripping and the occasional evening stay over, for a fee.

I was beginning to enjoy my strip nights and these began to include women's evenings and having to strip in front of them. I didn't find it problematic, except when some of them tried to grope me when I didn't want any groping at all. Had it been one of their boyfriends or husbands, then it would have been different.

It was some time during the summer that I received a strange call from a potential client. First it was strange in the sense that my grandmother took the call and the second, it was the nature of the request that made it strange.

"Chad, darling," called my Gran one afternoon. "I have a message for you."

"What's it Gran?"

"A strange lady phoned. She wouldn't give her name, but the message seemed odd. What do you do at night, my boy?"

When my grandmother asks questions like that, then I panic.

"Why, Gran?"

"She asked if you could call round to her house tomorrow night."

I wasn't sure whether to pursue the conversation or just ignore the message, but my Gran persisted.

"She said something about wanting you to perform for her," continued my Gran, her eyes somewhat like spaceships, wide and large. "Does your mother know what you do, whatever it is?"

"It's probably a party she's having and she wants a DJ to play the music," I offered as a story just to placate my grandmother.

"Didn't sound like that to me," she retaliated.

Now I really was beginning to worry that my folks, through my Gran, might find out what I was doing at night.

"No, Gran, that's what I do. A DJ is a disc jockey; the guy who plays the music at the parties, so that's probably what she meant about performing for her."

My Gran shook her head as if to say she never believed a word I was sprouting to her, and the look was equally disdainful. She gave a loud grunt in desperation and walked off to her room.

"So what else did she say," I shouted after her, but she chose to ignore me.

I saw a piece of paper lying next to the telephone with a number written on it, so I presumed it might be the so-called woman that Gran was talking about. I picked up the handle of the phone and dialed the number. It rang about three times and then I heard a man's voice on the other end.

"Hello," said the voice. "Can I help you?"

"Hi, my name's Chad and somebody at that number phoned me but I don't know what it was about," I said, sounding extremely vague.

"Well it certainly wasn't me," said the male voice.

"Apparently it was a female voice."

"Could have been my wife, but who are you and what do you do?"

"Sorry, sir, my name's Chad and I'm a DJ in my spare time, so I wondered if she had phoned about playing the music at a party, perhaps."

There was a moment of silence at the other end of the line and then the male voice continued.

"I'm not aware of any party, so I can't think why she would phone you."

I was beginning to think that perhaps he might think that I was some little lover of his wife and that we were having an affair behind his back.

"Hold on while I call my wife."

I heard him shout her name, Claudia, and I waited while she came to the phone.

"Hello," said a soft-sounding feminine voice.

"Hi, ma'am, my name's Chad and I think you phoned my number earlier but I wasn't available and my grandmother tried to take a message, but I think she didn't understand you properly, so that's why I've phoned back."

"Oh yes, yes, yes," she said, laughing as she said it. "I'm having a few friends around and I believe you do a very good strip show, so I was wondering if you'd be available to perform here."

"I'm flattered that you think so, but who mentioned my name to you?"

"My hairdresser," replied Claudia.

"Oh," I answered, not knowing who her hairdresser was.

"Well, would you be willing to perform for us; it's tomorrow night."

There was silence on the line while I contemplated the invitation.

"Um, before I say yes, we need to discuss fees," I said, with confidence.

I suddenly realized what I'd said and thought, 'hell I've got balls to say that.'

"Naturally, Chad. How would $500 for the performance be?"

I was stunned. I had never been offered so much money to take of my clothes, but I was not about to turn down that amount, so I agreed.

"There's just one thing extra," said Claudia.

I knew there had to be a catch. Getting this much money wouldn't be easy, so I waited to hear the caveat.

"Chad, I want you to do it in leather and I want the full house."

"When you say full house …"

"I mean you take everything off and we see what you've got," replied Claudia.

Normally at female parties or mixed ones, I always covered my private parts with my hands once I was naked, but now she wanted the 'Full Monty'.

Once more the line went quiet.

"Is it a deal?" purred the seductive voice of Claudia.

$500 was a great deal of money to a young man like me, especially as I wasn't working full-time. I thought about my assets and knew that I was well endowed and so I wasn't embarrassed by the size of my cock, so I agreed.

"Wonderful," cooed Claudia. "Have you got a piece of paper to write down my address?"

I grabbed a piece of paper and a pen and waited for the street address. As she gave it to me, I wrote it down, thinking all the time of the $500. The following evening at precisely 8:00p.m I would be at 652 4th Street entertaining Mrs. Claudia Hamilton.

With a sense of excitement I replaced the telephone handle and stood staring at the small piece of paper.

"What have you got there, Chad," said my mother as she suddenly appeared as if out of nowhere.

I wondered if she'd been standing listening to my conversation, but then I thought she was too much of a lady to eavesdrop on other people's conversations.

"Your Gran says she took a message for you."

"Yes, I got it thanks, Mum. That's why I made a phone call."

"Are you going out tonight, then?"

"No, tomorrow night. I have a date."

"A date! That sounds interesting."

"No Mum, not that sort of date. I have a DJ date; you know playing the music at a party."

"Oh," came the rather unexpectedly deflated reaction.

I think my mother was hoping I might have a date with a girlfriend. I didn't really have time to stand and debate the merits or demerits of having a girlfriend with my mother, as I had to get myself some sort of leather outfit for my performance the following night; but where?

Phone Greg, I thought. Maybe he knows someone who might have some leathers; but I couldn't phone from home because I was sure my mother or grandmother would hear me and then my cover would be blown. Unperturbed, I headed off to a callbox situated about two blocks from our house. I dialed Greg's number and when the phone was answered, I heard a woman's voice: it must have been his 'wife'.

"Hi, is Greg there, please?"

"Sure, hang on. Greg, there's a call for you."

I heard him ask who it was.

"I don't know but he sounds nice."

I was flattered to hear that I sounded 'nice'

"Hi there, Greg speaking."

"Hi Greg, it's Chad. I'm sorry to phone you at home like this, but I need some help," I said, almost whispering.

"Why are you whispering?"

"Wasn't that your wife that answered?" I enquired.

"Yes, but what difference does that make? What's the problem?"

"I have to do a show and I need to be dressed in leather, which I obviously don't have. Do you know anyone who's got some leather outfits?"

There were peals of laughter as Greg heard my plea.

"Don't laugh, this is serious."

"Sorry," replied Greg, pulling himself together. "I've got leathers if you want to borrow something."

"Have you," I answered excitedly.

"Sure, but when do you need them?"

"Tomorrow night. Is there any way you can get them to me?"

"Just come round to the apartment; you know the address."

"And what do we tell your wife when she meets me? That I'm some lost cousin of yours, or something like that?"

"Of course not. You're a friend, that's all. Now get yourself round here."

I slammed down the phone and hailed the first cab I saw and headed off to Greg's apartment.

When I arrived there I was met by a fairly pregnant wife at the door.

"You must be Greg's wife," I said, not showing too much interest in the fact that she was pregnant and they had only recently got married, even though I knew their set-up.

"Come in," she replied, charmingly. "Greg, your friend's here," she shouted into the unknown space.

Greg soon appeared and I was glad to see him again. He was dressed casually, but looked sexy and I felt a quiver in my groin when I looked at him.

"Hi, Chad, come on in and I'll show you what I've got, then you can choose."

I smiled at the thought that I knew what he had – a nice ass and a tasty cock, but I wasn't there for that. We went into his bedroom and there on the bed lay a variety of leather objects.

"I just laid out everything I've got in the form of leather and then you can pick what you want."

The first thing I picked up was a harness and looked at that.

"I would suggest you take that as you don't want to wear a shirt. It's better to show of your fine chest with the harness," said Greg, taking it from me and beginning to show me how to put it on.

"And this?" I asked pointing to a metal ring attached to the lower part of the harness.

"That's your cock ring. Put the harness on first and pull your cock and balls through the ring, then put the leather jockstrap on over it," suggested Greg. "Better still," he hurriedly added, "do you have a G-string, because you could put that on first and then put the jockstrap over it. Then you've got two things to peel off."

I thought that a good idea, after all, there's only so much leather that one can wear and take off.

"Try these jeans on," said Greg, handing me a pair of leather jeans he'd put out for me.

I whipped off my jeans and slipped into his. They fitted like a dream.

"Hm!" said Greg, parading around me, looking at the model. "That looks pretty hot on you," he added, slapping my ass. "And tight too!"

I felt the snug fit and decided that when I had made enough money, I'd invest in a pair of leather jeans like Greg's – they felt not only comfortable, but made me feel sexy and horny. I could feel myself becoming aroused. As I slipped out of the leather jeans, I noticed that I had a hard-on and so did Greg notice it.

"You like those, don't you, Chad," said Greg smiling at the bulge in the front of my briefs.

I tried to hide my hard-on, but to no avail, and merely giggled at having been caught out. I quickly pulled on my jeans in case Greg's wife walked in and saw my state, and we continued to try out all the bits and pieces of leather accoutrement. Once Greg had 'dressed' me so to speak, we packed the clothes into a bag and I set off back home, leaving both Greg and me a little hornier than before I arrived at his apartment.

Back home, Gran was in the lounge when I walked through and saw the bag.

"Leaving home, are you?" she asked cynically.

"No luck, Gran, but I'll let you know when I do."

"What's in the bag?"

You must understand, although I love my grandmother dearly, she really is the most inquisitive person I know, and if I had told her it contained leather clothing, I shudder to think what would have gone through her poor little mind. In Gran's day any mention of leather material would probably have been associated with furniture and not sexy clothing.

"It's just a bag, Gran."

"I can see that, but what's it for? We've got plenty of bags here without bringing home another one."

I decided not to get involved in this Spanish Inquisition, but rather head straight to my room where I hastily unpacked the bag and hid the clothes in my cupboard.

The following day, after having put on the entire outfit and worked out which bits of clothing would come off and in which order, I put them all back in Greg's bag and readied myself for the show that evening.

At 7:00p.m, the cab arrived and I said goodbye to my parents and headed off to Mrs. Claudia Hamilton's house, not quite knowing what to expect.

On arrival, I rang the front door bell and it was answered by their maid who ushered me upstairs to a bedroom.

"Madaaam weell be here soon, sir," said the maid, with a glint in her eye.

I wasn't sure whether the glint was because she knew what was in store for the evening, or whether she had taken a fancy to me.

I placed the bag on the floor and looked around the bedroom. It was luxuriously furnished and could have been a room for a girl or a boy as its décor was positively neutral. As I was busy admiring a painting on the wall, which thankfully, was one of those modern abstract painting that take hours or weeks to try and fathom out, the bedroom door opened and a charming, middle-aged woman appeared.

"Hello, I'm Claudia Hamilton," she said, extending a thin arm and hand in my direction.

I shook her hand and felt the firm grip and saw the smile –
it was a smile unlike any I had seen before. I wasn't sure if it was
because she had obviously had a face-lift and had difficulty smiling,
or whether it was just one of those evil looking smiles. I gave her the
benefit of the doubt and decided it must be the face-lift.

"Chad," she said firmly, "this is your room for tonight. You
may get changed in here and at precisely nine o'clock Maria, the
maid, will call for you and bring you down to the party where you can
do your show. After you have performed, she'll call a cab for you and
you may go."

This sounded so militaristic that I really became a little worried
as to what I might have got myself into.

"Certainly Mrs. Hamilton."

"Oh, and another thing, no drinks! I don't want some drunken
performance, not when I'm paying good money for it."

"Of course, Mrs. Hamilton."

With that, she turned on her high heels and strutted out of
the room, slamming the door behind her. I sat down on the bed, not
knowing whether to laugh or get the hell out of there and forego the
money. I wondered if she might be some re-incarnation of the *Adams
Family.* I opened the bag and pulled out my clothes, but as I still had
plenty of time, I decided to dress slowly.

I pulled off my shirt and sat on the bed, still trying to fathom
out the modern art on the wall. I had looked at the painting from
all angles and even bent over to look at it upside down but had no
idea what it was supposed to be. Having given up on the painting, I
slipped out of my jeans and briefs and pulled on the harness. Before
I gave myself a hard-on, thinking about the erotic feel the leather
gave me, I squeezed my balls and cock through the cockring and then
tightened the harness over my chest. I had planned that this was the
only thing that would not be taken off as it enhanced my chest and
the cockring would lift my balls and cock, enhancing them, especially
as Mrs. Hamilton wanted a 'Full Monty' performance. I then pulled
on a black satin G-string that I had found among my underwear.
Where I had got that from, I cannot remember, but it was coming
in handy tonight. Over that, I pulled on Greg's leather jockstrap and

immediately I felt myself get aroused. I don't know if it was the feel of the leather or the tightness around my bare ass, or even the fact that it was Greg's I imagined his cock lying in the comfort of the leather; but I got a hard-on. As I stood there admiring myself in the mirror on the dressing table, the bedroom door opened. A tall, sturdy looking African-American man stepped into the room. On seeing me in my outfit, his eyes grew wider.

"I'm sorry," said a softly spoken voice.

I spun around not realizing that the visitor could see that the package I had in the front of the jockstrap was groaning to escape. We stood and stared at each other. He was casually dressed, and had on a pair of well-fitting chinos which seemed to mould to his skin and a well-fitting shirt unbuttoned to reveal a smooth, dark many chest.

"I'm sorry to disturb you," he said, eventually. "I'm Mr. Hamilton. I take it you're tonight's entertainment."

"Yes," I replied, now trying to cover my erection with my hands.

"Well I can see my wife and her friends will get something very nice to look at tonight," continued Mr. Hamilton.

"Thank you for the compliment, sir," I stammered.

"Is that what you're wearing for them?"

"Yes, sir."

"Very impressive. I'm sorry that I won't be able to see the show; you know, it's ladies only," he said, coming into the bedroom and closing the door behind him. "And you are…?"

"I'm sorry sir. My name's Chad."

I released my grip on my crotch and shook the tall man's hand. I could feel warmth generate between us and suddenly didn't mind being seen with a roaring erection in my jockstrap.

"Well, make yourself at home, young man and I hope you have a wonderful show tonight, and I hope I see you around again."

With that he exited as quickly as he'd entered.

Not bad looking, I thought – nice body; tapered yet sturdy legs and from what I could make of the upper torso, probably had a chiseled chest. In fact – sexy.

By the time Maria the maid arrived at 8:55 p.m, I had lost my erection and was as nervous as anything about the show. Maria escorted me downstairs, grinning at me as she did so, until we reached a set of large wooden doors. From behind the doors, I could hear laughter and screams from female voices.

"How many people are there?" I asked Maria, tentatively.

"Ooh about tree hundred," she replied with her accented voice.

Panic set in, but then subsided because I didn't believe that three hundred people could fit into the lounge where I was to perform. Maria peeped through the door and obviously caught the eye of Claudia Hamilton, because no sooner had they made eye contact, than Mrs. Hamilton's voice boomed over all the others and she introduced the night's entertainment. Once she had announced what was coming, my music belted out and the large wooden doors opened and I entered.

Shrieks, screams, whistles and applause greeted me as I entered and started my routine. I danced, wriggled my hips seductively, thrust my crotch at people, sat on women's laps and generally began to relax. I could see there were only about fifty women in the room, but it still seemed like 'tree hundred'.

At a point, I placed my foot on a chair and seductively began to unzip my boots. Before I had a chance to complete the task, a lady nearby grabbed hold of the zipper and finished the job for me, so I let her do the same to the other boot. With my boots off, I was now able to get out of my leather jeans and down to the jockstrap. As I bent over to get out of my jeans, and with my bare ass, except for the black straps of my jockstrap showing, I felt the tingling sensation of a whip hit my ass. I immediately stood up with my jean around my ankles, to find Mrs. Hamilton on the floor with a cat-o-nine-tails type whip, brushing over my bubble-butt. Although the feeling was erotically exciting, I got a shock at seeing her there. I managed to get out of my jeans without falling over and continued my routine, trying to avoid Mrs. Hamilton's advances with her whip. I rushed to where an elderly lady was seated and sat on her lap, not to cool my ass, but to protect it from Mrs. Hamilton. I felt the lady's hand slid around to my crotch and felt a piece of paper being thrust into the jockstrap pouch alongside my cock. I looked down and saw a $50 note stuck there. Immediately I leapt up and moved to another area, where soon I was receiving more notes in the waistband of my jockstrap.

The time for the jockstrap to go arrived but this time, instead of turning my back on the women and getting it beaten by Mrs. Hamilton, I faced them front on and slid my jockstrap off. There was once more cheers and screams. Some of the money fell to the floor and I left it there because I still had to get rid of my satin G-string. The dance continued and more money got stuffed into the G-string pouch, but it was becoming awkward as my pouch was already bulging from my natural attribute, so there wasn't much more room for hands and money to be stuffed in there.

Finally the 'Full Monty' moment arrived. This time I did turn my back on them, but kept looking over my shoulder for Mrs. Hamilton and her whip as I slowly slid the G-string to the ground. I quickly glanced down at my balls and cock, tightly held in the cockring and was satisfied that they would make any person smile with joy, and spun around. The applause and screams was deafening to say the least and although I was naked for all to see, I was proud of my body and what I'd been blessed with. Money was now being thrown onto the floor and one middle-aged lady took it upon herself to run onto the floor and start collecting the money. Once she had collected it all, she ran up to me, handed me the cash and kissed me, but not before she made a grab for my cock and gave it a squeeze, to which she received a thunderous applause from the other ladies. With that, I fled through the large wooden doors and headed back to the bedroom.

I quickly pulled on my briefs and jeans to retain some dignity and very soon I heard a knock on the door. It was Maria.

"Come in," I shouted.

Maria entered, looking flustered and flushed.

"Choo good! Choo good and choo beeg!" she exclaimed excitedly.

I grinned at her as I put my money in the bag alongside Greg's leather clothes.

"Thee madam, shee's happy," continued Maria, gushing over me and trying to touch me.

She then handed me an envelope and said that the cab was waiting. I quickly finished getting dressed and headed downstairs to the cab. Once I was in the cab on my way home, I opened the envelope and there was my payment of $500. I looked at the tips that I'd received from the other women and realized I'm made a killing financially. I was so happy, that I asked the driver of the cab to take me to one of the bars in town before going home.

We stopped at a bar and I paid the driver, then went into the bar and ordered a beer. I was sitting quietly reminiscing about the evening's event, when out of the corner of my eye I saw a strikingly handsome man sitting alone in a corner of the bar. Somehow his face looked familiar, but as this was a gay bar, I didn't recognize him as one of the local gay guys. I picked up my beer and the bag and wandered over in his direction. It wasn't until I got up close that our eyes met and both of us looked embarrassed.

"I'm sorry, Mr. Hamilton, I didn't realize it was you here."

"Chad, what are you doing here?"

Now I was curious to know why he was there, but I thought it improper to ask.

"I finished the show at your place and I thought I'd like a drink, sir."

"I hope it went well for my wife," he replied, "and that you weren't molested too much by those crazy friends of hers."

I laughed, knowing what I'd been through, but financially, it was worth it.

"I survived, sir."

"I'm glad to see it. Would you like to join me for a drink?"

"Thank you sir that would be great."

I sat down at the small table next to him and he bought me another beer along with the martini he was drinking.

We sat smiling at each other and then Mr. Hamilton broke the ice.

"Do you do this sort of thing often?"

"Well I graduated from High school last year and I didn't want to go to college, so I hung around a bit and one thing led to another and soon I found I was being invited to strip at parties."

"And do you enjoy doing it?"

"It gives me an income."

"But you must work out, don't you? I mean, you have to have a good body for this sort of thing, don't you?"

"I suppose so, sir, but I don't work out."

"And I suppose the women want a guy who's… well you know…?"

"You mean well-hung."

"Yes."

"I suppose so, sir."

"So I take it you fit the ideal?"

"If you put it like that, sir, I'm told I'm pretty well-hung."

Mr. Hamilton smiled when I answered him.

We had a couple more drinks and then he offered to give me a lift home, which I gladly accepted. On the way home, he made a detour and headed to the town's park. We found and isolated spot and he switched off the motor. There was silence around us. The only light that was around us was from a clear moon shining down through the trees. Mr. Hamilton turned tome and smiled. With his eyes fixed on mine, I felt his hand slide onto my crotch and feel for my cock. His touch felt magnetic; it was soft and gentle as he found my cock and stroked along the denim material of my jeans.

"Mm! you do feel like a big boy, and by the feel of it, you seem to be a growing boy."

His touch was ending shivers through my body and I could feel my cock becoming harder and harder with each touch. I stretched my hand across to his chinos and could feel that he was fully aroused. He was no junior in the crotch department.

"You want to taste Daddy's meat," he said, unzipping his fly and pulling his long, thick cock out into the light.

I looked down at his length and saw how the head glistened in the moonlight from the pre-cum that had been leaking from his tip. He placed a hand behind my head and pulled my head closer to his throbbing cock. My mouth opened as I neared it and slowly swallowed his shaft as my lips met the tip of his cock. Very slowly, to begin with, he moved my head up and down as I sucked on his thick shaft, enjoying every mouthful I received.

He 'oohed' and 'aarghed' each time my mouth sank to the base of his cock and then he began to thrust his cock upwards, almost impaling my throat with his weapon. The only sounds that emanated from the car was his gentle moaning and heavy breathing and the occasional slurping sound my mouth around his cock, that is, until I felt the start of a barrage of sweet-salty cum entering my throat and then his moans became gasps and groans and his thrusts became frantic attacks on my throat and mouth. I retained the tight clamp on his shaft and sucked until I had drained him of every last drop of his warm see, then I slowly released my grip and licked his cock until it was clean of evidence. As I looked up into his face, I was met by a grinning, happy man.

"Not even my wife is as good as that, my boy, I can tell you that you have made Daddy a very happy man tonight."

I'm sure I blushed in the moonlight.

"I'm glad to have made both you and your wife happy tonight, sir, but in different ways."

"I would be very happy to meet you again, but you must never divulge to anyone where we met. I'm a high profile business man with a reputation to uphold, but I'm glad I went to that bar tonight."

"May I ask you something, sir?"

"Sure."

"If I hadn't pitched up in the bar tonight, would you have gone with someone else?"

"Let's just say, I'm glad you came along and leave it at that."

We sat smiling at each other in the car, neither saying anything, until I suggested that I get going.

"Before we go, would you mind if I asked you a question, Chad? It is Chad, isn't it?"

"Yes, sir."

"I'm not good with names, usually, and please call me Josh.

"Sure, Josh."

"You said earlier that you had finished high school and that you weren't doing anything with your life, is that right?"

"Yes sir. It's only the stripping that brings in money for me."

"I see. And tell me have you given any thought to your future?"

"You mean about a full-time job?" I asked.

"Yes, you could say that."

"No, not really sir,"

"You know there are a lot of young men like yourself who have good looks and fine bodies who make a great deal of money with their attributes."

"I'm sure there is, sir."

"Have you ever thought of branching out into movies or something like that to make more money?"

The idea had never entered my head, but having never done any acting, who was likely to hire me?

"You see, I have a small company that produces small budget films and maybe you might be interested," continued Josh.

"Sounds interesting," I replied, my mind racing through dollar signs. "But what sort of movies?"

"Let's just say art films," said Josh, smiling broadly at me. "Would you be interested?"

"Sounds like a good idea."

"Well how about meeting me tomorrow, if that's OK with you and I can show you what we do and give you more details."

Obviously the idea excited me; possibly my name in lights, fans thronging to get my autograph and men throwing themselves at my feet.

"Can you meet me tomorrow afternoon; say 3:30, if that's fine with you, Chad."

"That sounds fine, sir."

Josh gave me the address and added not to mention anything to his wife, should it ever arise, which I thought strange. He then started up the car and we drove back to my place, him looking happy and me like a child filled with excitement having receiving a gift. At the gate to our property, I thanked Josh for bringing me home and he thanked me for the service I had given him and then he drove off.

Gran was sitting up when I went indoors.

"Who was that, son?" she asked.

Oh dear! I knew I was in for another interrogation.

"The host of the party that I was a DJ for," I replied, hurrying to my bedroom and leaving Gran with a multitude of unanswered questions.

I undressed and collapsed onto my bed in the darkness of my room and thought about the whole evening and the offer that Josh had made.

CHAPTER 4

DRAMA AT HOME

The day after I had met Josh, I caught a cab to the address he'd given me and found myself in a rather downtrodden area of the town. There were storage sheds and a few sidewalk cafes of a dubious nature and a lot of rough looking people wandering around the streets. Both the cab driver and I seemed to have wondered if we'd wandered onto a nightmarish film set.

"Are you sure this is the right place, kid," asked the driver seeing my panic expression.

"It's the address I was given," I said, re-checking the piece of paper on which the address was written.

"It looks a bit of a dubious area for someone like you," he continued.

We had stopped outside a warehouse with a sign that read *Hamilton Enterprises.* I assumed it was the right place, knowing that Josh's surname was Hamilton, so I paid and got out of the cab. I wandered to the only door that I could see and opened it. It definitely felt a great deal cooler inside than out in the baking heat of the street. Once inside, I saw that the warehouse had been partitioned off to create smaller areas. Alth0ough I could faintly hear noises coming from the building, I couldn't make out specific noises, so I wandered in the direction in which I had heard some sounds. I came to another door and opened it. This led to an office in which sat a rotund African-American, smoking a cigar.

"Yeah!" he grunted, a cloud of smoke escaping from his lips as he spoke.

"I…I'm sorry to disturb you, sir, but I was looking for Mr. Hamilton."

"Through there," he said, pointing to another door that led off his office, "but he's not there. What's it in connection with?" asked the rotund man.

"He was going to show me around. He said something about making films," I said.

The man looked me up and down, but no facial reaction was forthcoming; it was more like a visual interrogation. The man was short but stout and although bald, he wore a toupee, which made him look almost comedic. The funny side of me kicked in and I hoped a gust of wind would suddenly appear and blow the hair off his head, but as I don't possess magical powers, nothing like that was likely to happen.

"He's in one of the studios," said the fat man.

"Can I not go through and see him there?" I enquired, hoping to get away from this boring little man as fast as I could.

He heaved a sigh, probably because it meant he'd have to walk somewhere which might take effort, but he eventually relinquished and offered to show me where Mr. Hamilton was.

We wander through a variety of spaces, for that is the only way I can describe the warehouse layout, until we entered a room which resembled a film set. There were bright lights and cameras, along with a number of men, who were obviously the technicians.

"Quiet on set," boomed a voice.

My fat friend held a finger to his lips indicating that I'd better shut up if I knew what was good for me. I stood and watched as a naked man and woman romped around on a bed and then the man hoisted the woman's legs high into the air and rammed his cock into her. I must admit the sight was very erotic, but it was not what I was expecting would be in a normal film. The scene continued for a while until the booming voice shouted "CUT!"

My fat friend led me over to a corner where I found Mr. Hamilton sitting watching the scene being filmed.

"Ah, it's Chad, isn't it," he said, smiling at me and waving fatty away. "Come and sit here, next to me."

I did as I was told and sat next to him.

"Did you manage to see that last scene we shot?"

I assumed he was referring to the naked man and woman, so I said I had.

"I don't expect you to do that, my boy."

I breathed a sigh of relief as that was not what I expected.

"No, come with me and I'll show you what I had in mind," he said, getting out of his chair and leading me away from the set and into another room where there was a similar type of set.

"This is more what I had in mind for you."

I looked around and saw a group of men sitting around smoking and talking to one another.

"But sir, nothing seems to be happening."

"Don't worry about that; they having a short break and soon they'll be back at work."

Just then a siren sounded and everyone jumped to their places.

"Get Dean and Mike," shouted someone.

Two men appeared wearing bathrobes and wandered onto the set where they disrobed and climbed onto a single bed that made up most of the set. Both men had erections and the one positioned himself behind the other.

"When I shout action, I want you to slip slowly into him, Mike. Take it slow so that the camera can capture your cock sliding in. It's going to be a close-up. Right? ACTION!"

The guy called Mike, held the stem of his hard cock and aimed it at Dean's ass, pushing slowly forward until the head popped in and then he sank his shaft further until his balls lapped up against Dean's ass.

"Now slowly pull out and sink back in," commanded the director.

As I sat and watched I could feel myself becoming aroused. The two men were oblivious of those around them and they just continued to enjoy the pleasure they were giving each other. I sat fascinated by their actions and as I watched, out of the corner of my eye, I caught Mr. Hamilton watching me. When the director eventually shouted "Cut!" the two guys who'd been making out with each other got off of the bed, their cocks still hard, and went off to another room.

"Chad, let's go to my office and have a chat," Said Josh Hamilton, leading the way back to his office.

We passed through fatty's office where he was still puffing on his cigar and entered Mr. Hamilton's office. He ushered me in and closed the door behind us.

"Chad, please have a seat."

I sat in a chair across the large oak desk from Mr. Hamilton, who rested his elbows on the desk top and stared at me.

"What did you think of what you saw this afternoon?"

I wasn't sure what sort of answer he expected, but I thought I'd better tell the truth.

"I must admit, Mr. Hamilton, I thought you were into straight types of films, but those were scenes from porno, weren't they?"

Josh Hamilton grinned at me, his enigmatic face looking very handsome in the office light.

"Chad, what is pornography? What you saw today was no different from anything you might accidentally see if you walked into someone's bedroom, isn't it?"

"I suppose if you put it that way, yes."

"If someone were to have filmed you and me in my car last night, would you have considered that pornographic? I wouldn't. To me that was extremely sexy and enjoyable."

"So what is your point sir?"

"My question, rather than my point, is would you be interested in making a couple of movies with scenes like you saw today?"

I looked seriously at him and thought long and hard. One half of me thought of the money that I could earn, while the other half became worried if my parents found out. What would they say, and better still, what would they think of me?

"Chad, you're not a child any more. You have left school, and rightly so you should be working and earning a living, something that most independent adults do."

Again I went into a deep thought.

"But would I have to have sex with women, sir?"

"No! I want you only for gay films, Chad."

I felt a lot better knowing that. I had never had any urge or desire to bed a woman and although I liked them, sexually I was not turned on by them. But a good looking man could turn me on easily.

"What would the money be like, Mr. Hamilton?"

"Chad, Chad; I told you to call me Josh. The financial side of things we can negotiate."

"Well could you at least give me some idea as to what I might earn, because if it's not worth it, then I'm not prepared to do it?"

It was now Mr. Hamilton's turn to sit and contemplate. He looked me up and down, rubbed his chin, and then spat out an answer.

"I'll start you off on $1000 a picture and we can talk about possible increments at a later stage. How does that grab you?"

"Can I still carry on doing my stripping?"

"I don't think so Chad. You see you'll be contracted to me, so I would have to decide what you can and cannot do. Of course if I think your stripping might advance the promotion of pictures we make, only then I'll agree to it, but I'm afraid you won't be able to strip whenever you felt like it."

I was now in a bit of a dilemma as I knew that from his wife's party I had made pretty close to $1000 with her fee and the tips from the other women. I told Mr. Hamilton roughly how much I had made at his wife's party and said that to make one film I might earn the same amount.

"Is there no way that I could combine both jobs, or at least could I maybe make one film and see if I like it?"

Mr. Hamilton shook his head.

"I'll tell you what, Chad; there are other studios that make similar types of films. Go to one or two of those and see what they'll offer you. I'm sure that it'll be less than I'm prepared to offer."

The idea appealed to me as it allowed me to buy a little time before making a final decision.

"Thank you Mr. Hamilton, I'd like to do that. It's just that I don't want to be rushed into something that I might have regrets over at a later stage."

"Son, you take your time. You know where I live and you know where these offices are, so when you're ready, you call me," said Josh Hamilton, rising from his seat and crossing to my side of his oak desk.

He opened the office door and called fatty.

"Cedric, please show Chad out, will you?"

Cedric! What a name for such a person. Cedric enveloped himself in a cloud of cigar smoke, coughed a couple of times, spat onto the concrete floor and heaved his heavy frame up out of his chair.

"This way," he muttered, leading me out of the office and escorting me out of the building.

I entered the brightly lit street. The sun was still blazing down and nothing had changed in the street. The people and the buildings remained forlorn and seedy. I hailed the first cab I saw and headed back to civilization, my home.

"Where have you been?" asked my mother, when I returned home.

"Out, Mum."

"Well, that's obvious."

"Why what's wrong?"

"Because people having been phoning all afternoon. And tell me what is this about strippers?"

I must have blushed when I heard the word. I didn't know how much she knew or what she was referring to.

"What about strippers?" I asked nonchalantly.

"You tell me."

There was a deathly hush as mother and son eyed each other.

"Are you stripping at parties, Chad?"

I couldn't lie to my mother; my Gran, maybe.

"Yes, Mum. I do it to earn money."

"Why can't you get a normal job like everyone else? Do you know how degrading it is to tell people that your son is a stripper?"

"But Mum, you haven't had to tell anyone as you've only just found out."

"Don't get cheeky with me my boy."

"I'm not being cheeky. Mum, it's a job like any other job and at least I'm not robbing banks or hold up people to rob them."

"I think it's disgusting," said my mother, venom almost spurting from her lips.

"But Mum, I'm not doing anything wrong. I'm earning money without having to beg for money and I'm bringing a bit of joy to people."

"What! Seeing you naked?"

I dreaded to think what my mother would say if she knew I'd been offered work in a porno movie. I also knew that arguing with her would be fruitless, so I headed to my room and closed the door behind me. I lay on my bed, thinking about what my mother had said, and what Mr. Hamilton had offered. As I lay there thinking, I heard a slight knocking on my bedroom door, which I chose to ignore. The door then opened slightly and I saw my Gran peering round the door at me.

"May I come in, Chad dear?"

I didn't respond, but that didn't deter my grandmother, who entered and closed the door behind her. She crossed over to my bed and sat down next to me.

"Chad, what you do is your business and I don't like to interfere, but your mother seems very upset. She did tell me what the problem was but I'm not here to condemn you. I want you to know that although that sort of thing was not common in my day, I realize times change. It's not something I'm like to see, but she said that you were earning money for it."

I sat listening to my Gran and was extremely surprised that she hadn't condemned me to a life in hell, but if I told her of Mr.

Hamilton's proposition, I'd be winging my way to the steamy depths of a fiery inferno, so I kept my mouth shut.

"Why don't you look for a decent job, my boy?" continued Gran, desperate to get me onto the straight and narrow.

"I don't see anything wrong with this type of work, Gran. I make good money and I enjoy it."

"Well, maybe, but money isn't everything," she retorted.

"Well, then, how would you feel if I earned nothing? I don't expect Mum to look after me and pay for everything. I want a bit of independence, Gran."

"I'm sure you do. It's just the nature of the work that I think upsets her."

My Gran continued trying to persuade me to give up my 'career' as a stripper, but having seen how much money I was getting for taking off my clothes, it was very difficult to give up the idea. I then realized that to keep the peace between my Mum and me, it would be better if I left home then I could do as I pleased without questions being asked.

"I'll think about it, Gran," I said, hoping to end her perseverance.

It worked, because soon after I said I'd think about it, Gran left my room and it gave me time to set my mind right. I enjoyed what I was doing but at the same time, I didn't want to upset my mum, so I thought I'd approach Mr. Hamilton and see if he couldn't arrange alternative accommodation for me and maybe I could work for him.

I spent most of the rest of the day and early evening in my room and when my Gran called me to dinner, I opted to forgo my meal, but remained in my room. I knew I'd be missed at the dinner table and I wasn't wrong. A knock came on my bedroom door and I heard my mother's voice.

"Chad, come down and eat your dinner."

I ignored the invitation and a little while later, my dad walked into my room.

"Chad, I need to speak to you. You've obviously upset your mother and I don't particularly want to hear the details, but at least come down and have your dinner."

I had always respected my father; not that I disrespected the others in our family, but my dad had never interfered in my life. I found that whatever I did, he always supported me, and I didn't expect anything different now.

"Dad, I don't know what Mum's problem is? She seems more concerned about what the neighbors are likely to say than worrying about how I feel."

"Look my boy, you know I've never stood in your way about things that you do, and personally, if you enjoy taking off your clothes for people, then I can't stop you. The only thing that would worry me is if you were being abused by people and not paid or things like that."

"Thanks dad, I respect your views. Do you know how much money I make by doing this?"

"No. I haven't any idea."

"At the last party, I came away with just about $1000."

"As much as that," said my dad, surprised by the amount. "Do you think they'd be interested in an old man like me taking off his clothes?"

What I loved about my dad was that I had inherited his sense of humor.

"Give it a try, Dad."

He roared with laughter at the suggestion.

"I don't have your looks or body, my boy."

"But you're not old," I said, encouragingly.

I had always been close to my dad, so I thought I'd take a chance and see what he felt about me doing movies.

"Dad, can I ask you something, but I don't want you to get angry or say anything to Mum?"

My father's look was one of a man of doubt. I wasn't sure if he was expecting some traumatic statement from me, but for me it was a simple question.

"Dad, I met with a business man today and he offered me a job if I wanted it."

"That sounds great Chad. What sort of work did he offer you?"

I hesitated as I thought how to word my replay carefully.

"It's a job in the movie industry."

My dad's expression changed to one of absolute joy.

"So you're going to be a movie star?"

"Maybe not," I responded.

"Well what then?"

"Yes, it is to act, but it's slightly more complicated."

My father's expression changed back to one of doubt.

I squirmed and shuffled myself around as I thought of a word to replace 'porno'

"Well… it's… uhm…arty films."

"Arty films! What do you mean?"

He was making it very difficult for me because I didn't know how he'd take it.

"I was asked to do a film that included sex in it," I stammered.

"SEX!"

"Yes, sex."

"And this, sex; is it in one scene in the film that you have to do it?"

"Uhm… that I don't know, Dad."

"What film is it?"

"Uhm… that's what I don't know…"

"You know you have to have sex, but you don't know what the film is? What are you talking about, Chad?"

I knew my dad was becoming confused and that was thanks to my inability to tell him exactly what I might end up doing.

"Are you talking about…porno," my dad whispered.

I must have blushed. No, I must have gone puce or scarlet or even neared death.

"So you're making a porno movie?"

I nodded and hung my head, but then a sudden idea sprang into my mind.

"I'm sure you've watched porno's before, Dad."

"Well… I… in my youth…"

I laughed at his embarrassment.

"You see you did!"

"Maybe, my boy, but I was never an actor in one of them."

"But I bet you wish you had been."

He smiled and it was so good to see that my dad was not about to eat me alive. That's why I like men; they always understand things.

Still laughing, my dad replied, "I don't know what to say, Chad."

"Let me tell you what I've thought. I don't want Mum to know, and I respect her views so I thought of moving out and getting a pad of my own then I can come and go as I please without offending any of you."

"You know I'd miss you if you did that, but I fully understand your situation."

To have my father's blessing was something I valued tremendously. I was also pleased that I'd been able to get the whole thing off my chest and be able to tell someone whose views I valued.

"Your food is getting cold," bellowed my mother's voice.

"I think we'd better get downstairs, my boy."

"But not a word to either Mum or Gran, please."

"I promise," said my dad, hugging me tightly. "Hell, I never thought I'd live to know a porn star," he muttered.

I laughed and the two of us ventured downstairs for dinner.

CHAPTER 5

MY FIRST TASTE OF FILMING

My father kept to his word and never told my mother the truth of my possible career, but he did explain how her young son needed to fly the nest and get an apartment of his own, so as to gain independence and start to earn for himself. At this stage, my father still didn't know one important aspect of the filming career: that it was going to be in gay porno.

Together with my dad, we found a small apartment on the other side of town, near to where Mr. Hamilton's studio was, except it wasn't in the industrial area and between us we collected some furniture – the basic type. The reason that my dad was helping me get started, was because my Mum had decided after the shock of stripping, she was washing her hands of me and my future. At least that's what her story was at the moment, but I was sure that sooner or later, she'd miss her only son and beg him to return home. Isn't that what mother's do?

During this time, I'd not made contact with Mr. Hamilton because I wanted to get myself on my feet and get my independence, but as soon as my apartment was furnished, I would contact him.

My dad put a fair amount of money into my bank account to make sure that I at least had something to start me off with and once he knew I was safely started on my film career, he left me to my own devices.

Throughout this period, I had never been able to get the list of phone numbers that my mother had taken the day this all blew up, so I had lost a fair amount of business. With this in mind, I contacted Mr. Hamilton.

"Glad to hear from you, Chad. It is Chad, isn't it?"

"Yes sir. I was wondering if the offer was still on."

"Oh, you mean about doing some films for me?"

"Yes, sir."

"Can you get around to the studio today because I have a slight problem; one of my actors has gone off sick and I need a replacement urgently."

I couldn't believe my luck, so I wrote down what time I was needed and what to wear. I know that sounds stupid, when you're naked most of the time having sex, but maybe the character might have to arrive at a setting with his clothes on.

As my new apartment was fairly close to the studio, I didn't have to get a cab. I wandered along the streets until I reached the studio, but as I did so, I noticed a few young men loitering along some of the streets. I knew exactly what their purpose in loitering was about and wondered how much money they made in a day.

When I arrived at the studio, fatty was there to meet me having been forewarned by Mr. Hamilton. I was hastily led through the various offices and corridors to the studio where Mr. Hamilton was waiting for me.

"I'm so glad you phoned," he said, shaking my hand. "I need you to fill in for one of my actors."

"Sure, sir, but we need to talk money first."

"Quite the little business man! I'll tell you what, let's shoot the scenes first then we can talk finances."

"Sorry sir, but I'd prefer to talk money first before I commit to taking part in the film."

"You drive a hard bargain, don't you, but I like someone like that. OK. I'll give you $800 for today's shoot and then can we negotiate a future fee?"

I pretended to contemplate his offer and I could see he was becoming agitated because he probably thought I was wasting his time.

"Ok sir, it's a deal," I answered.

"Right, let me explain what you're going to do."

There was no signing of contracts as I expected, but I was swept off to a smaller room with Mr. Hamilton, to be told of my part.

"I want you to put on this Speedo," he said handing me a skimpy white bathing costume, "and I think spray some tanning lotion onto yourself to bronze up the color of your skin a bit. Then I'll take you through to the set."

I peeled off my jeans, briefs and T-shirt and slid the soft Lycra Speedo on. I adjusted the lie position of my balls and cock and noticed how Mr. Hamilton watched with greedy interest. His eyes stayed fixed on the bulging crotch and I knew he could see the shape of my cock through the whiteness of the material. I picked up a towel that was lying on a chair in the change area, wrapped it around my waist, took up a bottle of bronzing tanning spray, and sprayed my chest, arms and legs. As I was unable to reach my back, I smiled coyly at Mr. Hamilton and handed him the bottle.

"Do you think you could do my back for me please, sir?"

I felt the cool spray hit my shoulders and back and equally suddenly I felt his hands drifting over my shoulders and back as he rubbed the tanning lotion into my skin. His touch was gentle and erotic, his finger tips gliding over my body, and as he did this, I could feel myself becoming aroused, but he could also see that, so his smile broadened. He led me through to a smaller studio in which was a pool lounger with a badly painted backdrop of a swimming pool area. As I surveyed the room, I saw another actor lying on the pool lounger, chatting casually to one of the cameramen.

"Let me introduce you," said Mr. Hamilton, crossing over to the pool lounger.

The man lying there was probably in his early thirties and had in his time probably been a body builder as his muscles bulged from every part of his body. He looked me up and down and saw my semi-erect bulge in the front of my Speedo and grinned at me.

"Has Josh been at you?"

I was dumbstruck by his statement and wondered why he'd said that, other than Mr. Hamilton probably made passes at all his actors.

"I'm not quite as bad as you, Mitchell, now let me introduce you. This is Chad, and he's replacing Troy. Chad this is Mitchell."

I nodded and so did he, but I noticed how transfixed he was on my crotch.

"Right gentlemen, we're going to take it from the top," said Mr. Hamilton, taking the role of director. "Mitchell, you're sprawled out on the lounger and Chad, when I give you the cue, I want you to wander into camera shot, hesitate when you see him and then start rubbing your hand across your crotch."

I nodded to show that I understood, and Mr. Hamilton then continued.

. "Mitchell, when you see Chad becoming aroused I want you to rub your crotch, but once you're hard, I want you to rub your hand in such a way so that it pulls down the waistband of your Speedo so that we can see the tip of your cock peeping over the top. When you see that, Chad, I want you to advance to Mitchell and kneel next to his lounger and start rubbing your hand over the revealed part of his cock. When I say so, I then want you to pull his Speedo down further so that you have complete access to his cock and then I want you to start licking and sucking his cock. Understood?"

"Yes, sir," I said, already knowing that my cock was getting harder by just thinking of what was going to happen.

"Right, places everyone," shouted Mr. Hamilton. "And, ACTION!"

I wandered into camera shot and started rubbing my already hard cock and very soon Mitchell was doing likewise. It didn't take him long to get hard and even sooner for his cock to peep over the top of his Speedo. When I saw the smooth head peeing out, my cock immediately began to throb. I moved closer and knelt next to the lounger and with trembling hands, I pulled his Speedo down to reveal his long, hard cock. I didn't need any invitation to take it into my mouth. It lay there begging to be taken, so I willingly obliged. My mouth tightened its grip around his thick shaft and Mitchell let out a low growl as I sank my mouth over his throbbing length.

Mr. Hamilton sat focused on my 'acting' skills, until he felt he'd watched enough.

"CUT!" He shouted. "That was pretty good you guys. Take a five minute break while we set up for the next scene."

"You're pretty good, for a kid," said Mitchell as he rose from the lounger, his hard cock bobbing in the air. "You done this thing before?"

"No, this is my first movie," I said, laughing, happy to have done something right.

"In the next scene I get to taste that sweet ass of yours," said Mitchell, slapping my ass.

I was somewhat concerned because Mitchell wasn't a small guy and I had visions of my poor ass being spilt from San Francisco to New York. Once Mr. Hamilton had re-arranged the set, he came up to me, patted me on the shoulder and complimented me on my performance.

"In the next scene, Chad, Mitchell's going to get your Speedo off you and start eating your ass. I want you to spread your legs as wide as you can so the camera can get between your legs to film upwards. Are we ready?"

I stood next to the lounger while Mitchell knelt behind me. When the magic word 'Action" was shouted Mitchell's tongue began to give my ass a good washing. I bent forward slightly to allow him easier access and felt his tongue delve deeper into my asshole. His hands parted my ass cheeks and his rough tongue grazed over my hole driving me crazy. I looked down and saw the camera facing up taking in my ass and Mitchell's long, sharp tongue at work.

"Cut!" shouted Mr. Hamilton. "I might come back to that scene, but at the moment it looks OK. Mitchell, I want to shoot the fuck scene then we'll do the cum shot. Chad do you need to go to the bathroom?"

"No, I'm fine thanks," I responded.

"In case you want to prepare yourself," whispered Mitchell.

I suddenly realized what he meant.

"Oh yes, thanks Mr. Hamilton."

I rushed off to the bathroom and got myself ready for Mitchell's invasion of my ass. When I returned, the crew was ready for me. I was a little apprehensive about getting fucked as I'd only been fucked by Fred and I knew that Mitchell was bigger than him. Although my ass had only been attacked once, I had to admit that I enjoyed the feeling and found that I was hoping that with Mitchell it would be the same.

"Guys," said Mr. Hamilton, bringing all conversations to a halt. "Get the condom on and the lube ready and I want you, Mitchell to be lying back on the lounger and Chad, I want you to stand astride his legs and slowly lower yourself onto his shaft, but it must be slow and we need to see your pucker quivering as he pushed into you."

"You don't have to worry about that Mr. Hamilton, my ass is quivering already from fear; the guy's a monster."

"Well slide on it and enjoy, is what I say," said the director, positioning himself where he could watch Mitchell's cock sliding in and out. "Are we ready? And, ACTION!"

Mitchell stroked his cock a couple of times as I positioned myself across his thighs, then I slowly sank down onto his massive cock. I felt it touch my asshole and I hesitated, then I attempted to slide down further, but I could feel the pain as his cock tried to push into me.

"Push down!" shouted Mr. Hamilton.

I did as I was told and I began to feel Mitchell break through my sphincter and then it was an easy slide into my tight tunnel.

"Aargh! I cried as the pain hit me, but ironically, out of this pain, there was an intense feeling of pleasure.

"Now ride him, Chad."

I grabbed onto Mitchell's plump nipples that extended up and out and squeezed hard on them. He growled like a hungry lion and thrust his cock deep inside me, lifting me high into the air and allowing the cameraman a good view of his cock embedded tightly in my ass. The more I pinched on Mitchell's nipples, the more rough his fucking became and at one stage I thought I would fly right off his cock, but throughout this, his cock never escaped the tight stranglehold my ass muscles had on his cock shaft.

"Fuck, you're getting me close," shouted Mitchell.

"Then stop," ordered Mr. Hamilton. "Have you guys got enough footage?" he asked the cameramen.

They muttered that they had and we were then given an instruction to 'take five'.

I realized what a let down filming was becoming. Every time I had got aroused and almost reached a point of no return, we'd be made to stop and then we'd have to start all over again. As we took our five minute rest, both our cocks subsided, but Mitchell continued stroking his in an effort to stay hard.

"Are we ready?" shouted the director, but on seeing my state, he was not amused. "Why are you so soft, Chad?"

I really didn't have an answer, but Mr. Hamilton did.

"Fluffer, get Chad hard again."

A young man, probably my age or thereabouts, rushed forward and sucked my cock into his mouth. At first I was startled until I realized that his actions were getting me hard again. He continued sucking until he felt that I was sufficiently hard for the shoot.

"Right everyone. Mitchell, lie back on the lounger and Chad stand astride him. You must both stroke your cocks and when you're ready to shoot, Chad I want you to shoot first and cover Mitchell's cock with your cum, only then must you come Mitchell by using some of Chad's cum to slick up your own. Get it?"

We both understood and began to do as we were instructed while the two cameramen wandered around us waiting for the explosive moment. It didn't take me long to reach my climax, thanks to the tight mouth of the fluffer and I duly shot my load over Mitchell's hand and cock. This set him off and he too was firing on all cylinders, with streaks of white liquid landing on his buffed chest and tight stomach. Our gasps and groans were the only sounds emanating from the room and when we'd exhausted ourselves, we smiled at each other and heard Mr. Hamilton shout "CUT!"

"That's a take," said the director. "You two go and clean up we're finished for the day. That was good work guys."

At that, Mitchell and I headed off to the make-shift showers.

"How was that?" enquired Mitchell.

"Wow, you were awesome," I answered, scrubbing the drying cum off my hands and legs.

"You've got yourself one helluva tight ass there, and a fucking good cock. I think you'll make it big in this business, Chad."

I was truly flattered by his comments and as the two of us stood under the cascading water, cooling down our tired bodies, so our cocks returned from a stimulating journey.

"Do you do many movies for Mr. Hamilton?" I asked Mitchell.

"I've done about twenty for him, but I did a few for another director before joining Josh."

"Tell me, what's his scene?"

"Meaning?"

"Well the first time I met him I was doing a strip show for his wife, so I was very surprised when he offered me work and in a gay porno movie."

Mitchell chuckled.

"Let's just say, Josh is bisexual. He gets plenty of sex from his wife, when she's in the mood, that is, but then he gets a lot from the guys."

"Can I ask you a personal question, Mitchell?"

He laughed out loud.

"Before you ask, the answer is yes."

"But you don't know what I'm going to ask."

"You want to know whether Josh and I have had sex together, don't you?"

"Well…"

"I told you the answer was yes; many times, as I'm sure you'll find out, if he hasn't already tried with you."

"I only gave him a blowjob once."

"Hey, the fact that you're here means you must have given him an awesome blowjob. Usually the guys only get offered parts when he's screwed them," replied Mitchell, switching off his shower and beginning to dry himself. "You see, Josh is very into white guys. He once said to me he thought white guy's asses were sweeter and tighter than guys of color, but that the guys of color's dicks were bigger than the white guys. That's debatable though, if you look at yours and mine."

I finished showering and also began drying myself, when Mr. Hamilton entered the shower area.

"Chad when you're finished please come to my office, will you?"

"Sure thing sir."

With that, Mr. Hamilton left for his office.

"What's with the sir thing?" asked Mitchell. "He's Josh."

"I don't know. I suppose it's just respect," I answered. "He did tell me to call him Josh, but I haven't got to know him properly yet to do that."

"So where do you stay, Chad?"

"I've just moved into a small apartment nearby."

"I thought you'd still be with your folks."

It was my turn to laugh, knowing what I'd been through with my Mum.

"I had a bit of trouble with my Mum, but my Dad was cool. He helped me move."

"Sounds like a decent sort of guy, your dad."

"Hey don't get me wrong, both my mum and dad are cool, it's just that my mother doesn't understand what I do."

"And your dad does?"

"Well he knows I've gone into the porno making, but he doesn't know it's gay."

"So you're still in the closet?"

"To my folks, yes, but to my friends, no."

"Well I'm not likely to meet either of your parents, so your secret's safe with me."

"What about you? What's your preference and are you in any sort of relationship?" I asked.

"It's often hard in this type of business to form a relationship, but I have been dating another actor for about four months."

"Is he also into porno movies?"

"Oh yes, you'll find they're the only guys whole date you. All the others don't want to have a relationship with you because they don't trust you. I don't blame them when you're fucking a different guy every day, or being fucked by one."

"I hadn't thought of it like that," I replied.

"You see my partner and I have an understanding; this is a job and there are no emotions involved. When I fuck a guy, I feel nothing, emotionally I mean, but when I get home and my partner and I have sex, then there's passion."

"I suppose I'll get used to it."

"Look it takes time and you have to be able to split the work from the social, but it is a profession where you can get hurt and badly."

"Have you?"

Mitchell suddenly looked forlorn.

"A long time ago."

"Why what happened?"

"I met a really cute guy who was also in the porno business and we started dating, but I didn't know that he had Aids and after being together five months, he died."

Immediately my mind flashed to our having sex together and I panicked that Mitchell might have Aids and pass it on to me. He noticed my concern, but was quick to allay any fears I might have had.

"It's OK kid, I'm tested regularly and I'm clean; you have to be tested regularly in this sort of business, but in any case we used a condom, so you've got nothing to worry about, but you must protect yourself in this business if you want a long career."

The smile that had covered my face earlier, returned.

"Why don't you come round this evening and meet Chris, he's my partner. Come and have dinner with us."

"That would be great, thanks Mitchell."

We finally got dressed and Mitchell wrote down his address and then as I made my way to Mr. Hamilton's office, so Mitchell went home.

I knocked on the office door and heard Mr. Hamilton's voice call me in.

"You wanted to see me sir?"

"Yes Chad. I wanted to say, well done. I think you did an amazing job today and I'd like you to know that I definitely will use you again."

"Gee, thanks Mr. Hamilton, I appreciate that."

"How did you like working with Mitchell?"

"I think he seems a decent sort of guy. Yeah, I liked working with him."

"So would you like to work with him again?"

"If he's happy working with me, sir."

"I'll speak to him. Now tell me, was that the first time anyone has penetrated you?"

It concerned me a little that the conversation was becoming somewhat personal and I wasn't sure where this was leading.

"Please don't take me too seriously. It's just that I need to know what sort of sex you like, so that when I match you up with other guys, I get it right."

"This was the second time for me sir, but I don't mind either way. Mitchell was very gentle with me and although he was considerably bigger than the first guy that penetrated me, I didn't mind him at all."

"I'm glad to hear that because I don't have many attractive and well-hung bottoms who can also act as a top. You see, if you're able to accommodate both positions, it makes your work options better."

"I enjoy both, sir, even though I've fucked more guys than have fucked me."

"Right, thank you for that. Now let's get down to the more important issue of payment. I promised you $500 for today's shoot, didn't I?"

I was taken aback but decided that perhaps he might have forgotten.

"Sir, I think you said $800," I replied, determined to get my money.

"Are you sure about that?"

"Absolutely, sir."

"Well, what if I give you $500 and a treat?"

"Sir, you said $800 for the shoot."

"I was hoping that you might consider spending some time with me as a treat."

"I think I'd rather take the money, sir."

"Are you rejecting my offer, Chad?"

"It's just that you said…"

"Most people would consider it an honor to have me treat them, especially when they were still unknowns and they knew that I could put them on the map to stardom."

I didn't like the idea of being ripped off, but I also didn't want to throw away my chances of a fruitful career.

"Why don't we go next door to the other studio and make a decision there. Come along Chad."

Mr. Hamilton led the way to the set that had a bed on it and I followed. By the time I reached the studio, he was standing naked next to the bed, his long, thick, dark cock hanging well below his pendulous balls and he was smiling.

"You know you were so good to me the last time we saw each other and you treated my cock with such loving care, that I wanted to thank you for that. Why not come here, Chad."

I moved slowly towards him, watching as he gently stroked his cock to life. When I reached him, I could feel his hot breath against my face and his lips caressed my neck. His hands manipulated my shirt buttons and soon I was shirtless. Then his fingers felt for my zipper and a warm hand was inserted into my jeans and my cock rose to meet it.

"My, that feels good," he cooed into my ear. "You're so hard, just like me. Feel it."

I stretched my hand down and felt the hardness of his thick cock and instinctively I started stroking it.

"Hm! That's delicious. Would you like to feel me slip inside of you and warm you tight little chute for you, Chad?"

By now my eyes were closed and I was nearing paradise. My jeans were shucked to the ground and I felt his warm hands cup my ass cheeks and then his fingers went in search of my crack and the rose pucker, waiting to be massaged. It didn't take his fingers long to find their target and he gently massaged my opening, causing me to relax so that his thick, stubby fingers could slide effortlessly into my asshole. He inserted first one, then two fingers and massaged my inside. When he felt ready, he slipped in another two fingers so that he had almost his whole hand in my ass, spreading it wider. Each time his hands penetrated my ass, I relaxed a little more until I was ready to be taken. My juices were flowing and Mr. Hamilton pushed my back forward so I was bending and then, taking hold of his thick shaft, he slowly advance into my pucker and sank deeper and deeper into my tunnel until his balls came to rest up against my ass cheeks.

Ooo, wow that felt good. His firm strong thrusts pushed me forward but I managed to remain bent over while his cock massaged my prostate and his hands my ass cheeks. His hands never veered near my cock, but I knew he was hitting home base because as he pumped my ass, so I got nearer and nearer to shooting my load. His breathing remained steady, but his pace increased and so did the depth into which he sank. His balls constantly slapped against my ass bringing him closer too. I then hear an increase in his gasps and groans and with the knowledge that he was close to shooting, I let go of my pent-up passion and forcing my ass back onto his cock, I fired the first of a volley of shots onto the floor of the set. As my ass muscles clamped tightly around his stiff column, I felt him tense and then the erratic throbbing of his cock started. I felt his load spewing into my guts and his breathing was loud and forceful as he plowed into me. When he was spent of his seed, he slowly pulled out of me, pulled me into an upright position, turned me around so our two cocks rubbed up against each other, and kissed me.

"Now let's get your $500."

CHAPTER 6

DINNER FOR THREE

I made my way back to my apartment, once again passing the young guys on the streets, plying their trade. A couple even made passes at me hoping I'd pick them up, but I was not in the mood for extra sex. I got home, and immediately showered as I was hot and sticky from walking in the heat which still lingered at the end of the day.

When I returned home, I'd found a note shoved under the front door to my apartment. I opened it and found that Dad had scribbled me a message, asking how my first few days alone had been. I was touched by his concern but couldn't tell him exactly what I was doing.

I dialed our home number and Mum answered.

"Hi Mum, how are you?"

"Hello darling, I should be asking you how you are. Are you OK?"

"I'm fine thanks Mum. Is Dad there?"

"Hang on, I'll call him."

I heard her shout into the distance and soon heard the footsteps as my Dad reached the phone.

"Hi son, how are things?"

"Hi Dad, thanks for the note. I've just got back home now."

"Are things fine with you and do you need anything?"

"No thanks Dad; I'm OK."

"How's the work going?"

I knew I'd have to be wary as to how I responded to work questions without compromising my situation.

"Not bad, thanks. I actually did some work today."

"That's great. What's the movie called?"

Oh dear, I didn't know what to say.

"They haven't finalized a title yet Dad," I quickly responded.

"So what's it about?" Asked my Dad, who was beginning to sound like my Gran.

I thought about that and realized that I had no idea what the film was about. Even though Mitchell and I had done some scenes together, I didn't even know if there were others in the movie, let alone knowing what it was about.

"Uhm … it's actually very difficult to tell, Dad, because they shoot scenes out of sequence."

"Well what did you have to do in your scene?" asked my enthusiastic father.

Oh shit, this was getting worse and worse. I couldn't very well say, 'Guess what Dad, I got fucked by a guy!' or could I?

"Listen Dad, there's someone at the door, can I call you back later?"

"Sure, son, just look after yourself then."

I replaced the telephone feeling as guilty as hell having lied to my dad, but what else was I to do?

I wandered into my bedroom and opened the cupboard to find some clothes to wear. I pulled out a pair of denim jeans and a T-shirt and slipped into them, deciding to go without underwear for a feeling of more freedom. I zipped up and pushed my cock down the left leg side, adjusted my balls and was ready to head for Mitchell's place. As he wasn't close by, I had to call a cab, which soon arrived. Having given the driver the address, we sped through the evening traffic and very soon arrived at the apartment block in which Mitchell and Chris lived.

It was a very imposing looking building because it had a stern doorman who looked me up and down when I entered the foyer, but once I told him where I was headed, he smiled and seemed a lot friendlier towards me.

I reached the twelfth floor and found the apartment number and rang the door bell. Mitchell answered the door and invited me in. He was wearing a pair of casual shorts and a vest which enhanced both his upper body and his muscular legs. He greeted me and led me into their finely decorated lounge.

"Chris, this is Chad," said Mitchell introducing me to his partner.

Chris looked younger than me, but as I was only nineteen, I didn't think he could actually be younger. He had a sweet, open face and short, cropped blond hair that framed his angelic face. He too was wearing shorts and a vest, similar to Mitchell's.

"Hi there, Chad. Mitch's told me a lot about you."

"I don't know if that's a good thing or not," I replied, sitting in an easy chair that Mitchell had shown me.

"He only ever says good things about his co-actors," continued Chris.

"What can I get you to drink, Chad?" asked Mitchell.

"Beer if you have, please."

"It's three beers then," said Mitchell as he departed for the kitchen.

"Mitch tells me this is your first movie. What do you think about the whole scene?" asked Chris.

"I'm excited about it and I really enjoyed today, but of course, my folks don't know anything about what I'm doing."

Chris laughed, and added, "Most parents very seldom ever find out. Mine have no idea, even though I've been doing this for about four years."

"But you look so young to have been in the business for four years."

Just then Mitchell re-entered the lounge with our beers.

"I like this guy," said Chris. "He knows how to flatter a person."

"Why what's he telling you?"

"He can't believe I've been in the business for four years."

"No," I interrupted. "It's not the four years, it's that you look so young to have been doing it for so long."

"You see how he flatters," continued Chris. "Chad, I'm twenty-three."

"Wow, you don't look it, Chris," I exclaimed.

"You see, Chris has been blessed with one of those faces that never seems to age, so he has the advantage of being all sorts of movies; such as those with twinks or teens as well as young guys. You see, for me, I'm beginning to be limited to movies involving older guys," said Mitchell.

"I can't believe it. You really have kept yourself looking young."

"Thanks. It's been an asset because I can then act in a variety of types of movies, and the funny thing is that Mitch and I have only been together in a couple of movies. He tends to get the leather, macho manly type and I get the young guy type movies. I don't mind, but I'd like to make more movies with him."

"Maybe when I get too ugly or too old to be in movies, I'll turn to directing and then I'll cast us together," replied Mitchell.

"In that case, I can't wait for you to get old!" chuckled Chris, hoping that he would get a crack from Mitchell.

"I'm glad you never said 'ugly'."

"You'll never be ugly in my eyes," retorted Chris.

"I was telling Chad that he must try to be versatile if he can because then his usage in movies becomes greater," said Mitchell.

"He's right there, but I prefer being a bottom," commented Chris.

"Have you never been a top?" I asked, sipping my beer.

"A couple of times in the twink type movies, but I don't enjoy it as much as being screwed by some heavy-hung dude."

Both Mitchell and I laughed at Chris's description.

"So am I a heavy-hung dude?" enquired Mitchell.

"Of course."

"Well, then you must see Chad. He's got some good equipment between his legs."

Chris's face lit up with delight.

"Chris, do you also work for Mr. Hamilton?"

"I did a couple of movies with him, but then I left and went to another company."

"May I ask why you left?"

"I just wasn't happy with his conditions."

"What sort of conditions are you talking about?"

"You see, if you're a bottom, you're an expendable commodity. Guys who are bottoms are two-a-penny so to keep your position, you have to be good looking, well-hung and willing to do anything."

"And which of those requirements don't you have?" I asked, tentatively.

"The willing to do anything."

It was at this point that Mitchell butted in to the conversation.

"You see, Chad, Josh as I told you, is very into white boys, but more so into young white boys, so he was always after Chris. At first Chris took it as part of the introduction to the company and being accepted, but then Josh got more demanding and Chris just felt he'd had enough."

"It would be every night that he'd keep me back in the studio and … you know…"

I remained silent throughout this time, until Mitchell spoke up again.

"How's he been treating you, Chad, although I know you're brand new to the company?"

I smiled almost cynically.

"Oh, he's started already; just this afternoon."

"When?" asked Mitchell.

"After you left, I had to go to his office, as you know. When I got there he said he was very happy with my performance today…"

"…and he was right," interrupted Mitchell.

"But when I asked for my money, he offered me $300 less than what he'd quoted me."

Mitchell and Chris looked at each other, as though they had experienced the same thing.

"I asked for the full amount and then he started backtracking and offered my less money plus a 'treat'."

"And the treat was a session with him?" suggested Mitchell.

I nodded.

"I suppose he fucked you and said it was worth the amount of money you were not being paid," asked Chris.

"Well not in so many words, but yes, I got the fuck."

"I'm sorry if I laugh," said Chris, "but he did the same to me."

"You see, Chad, he'll do it to guys who are new and uninitiated in the ways of the industry or guys who are effeminate and won't pout up a fight with him, but he never tries it with the butch guys," said Mitchell, understanding my situation. "What you have to do is either stand up to him or if you accept his conditions, then you shut up and do as you're told. That's why Chris left the company."

"But you're still there, Mitchell."

"Yes, but you see I'm older and I've been around a while. I think he's also scarred of my size, and I'm not talking cock here."

We all laughed and that broke the tenseness in the room.

"The only thing I'll have to do is try to get extra work to supplement my small income," I said, draining the last dregs from my beer bottle.

"Would you like another one, Chad?" asked Mitchell, rising from his seat.

"Thanks."

"What about you Chris?"

"Same again, please, and can you check the food in the oven?"

Mitchell exited again to the kitchen, leaving Chris and me alone.

"What were you doing before you started with the company, Chad?"

"Stripping."

"Oh wow. That must have been fun. Are you still doing it?"

"When I first met Mr. Hamilton, he did make it clear that I would have to give up my stripping if I worked for him."

"Don't take any notice of that. If you have to earn, then you do what you want. He doesn't own you, especially when he skims the money from you."

"Do you do any other work other than films?"

"I used to, but after I met Mitch, I stopped that."

"What were you dong?"

There was a slight pause before Chris answered.

"Hustling," came the reply.

"You mean…!"

"Yeah, I was prostituting myself, if you want to put it like that."

"What was it like?"

"Hey I made money, but the conditions under which you work can be traumatic, especially when you get those kinky kind that want to tie you up or beat you just so that they can have some pleasure at seeing you suffer."

"But you say the money was good?"

"Provided you have a good place to look for trade, such as a busy road and there isn't too much competition, but you have to be careful."

Mitchell entered with our beers and asked, "What are you too gossiping about?"

"We're not gossiping," replied Chris.

"I was asking Chris what he did before meeting you."

Mitchell sat down and put his arm around Chris's shoulder as if to comfort or protect him.

"That's past now, isn't it?"

Chris smiled and nodded.

I had never thought of hustling before, but Chris had planted a seed of thought in my mind. Maybe, just maybe I might make some extra cash from hustling, but I needed to be careful how I went about it. Maybe I could chat to some of the young guys who frequented the streets near the studio and find out what it was like in that area.

Dinner was ready, so we traipsed through to the dining room and settled down to Chris's dinner of roast and vegetables followed by ice cream and chocolate sauce. As we were eating, the telephone in the apartment rang, so Mitchell excused himself to answer it. When he returned he had a broad grin on his face.

"Looks like you're in work again, Chad."

Both Chris and I looked surprised.

"What are you talking about?"

"Apparently Josh was trying to get through to you and couldn't get hold of you, so he phoned me. He wants both of us at 10:00 tomorrow morning to shoot some other scenes for the movie."

"Different scenes or retakes?" I asked.

"No; different scenes."

"That should be a little extra money for you, Chad," remarked Chris.

"Josh is also bringing in the guy whose part you took. Apparently he had a problem and couldn't make the filming, but he'll be there tomorrow."

I imagined that if I had taken his place, he might be annoyed but also, it would have been him being screwed by Mitchell, so what was going to happen tomorrow? I think Mitchell noticed my trance-like look.

"What are you thinking, Chad?"

"Sorry, I was just wondering what the guy would think with me taking his part."

"Don't let that worry you. In Josh's system, if an actor is missing, he's quickly replaced. Nobody said it was his role. In any case, and I don't mean this in a derogatory way, but the guy put there is merely an ass to fuck. I'm sorry if it sounds coarse, but it's the truth. You were there so that I could complete the scene with someone to ride my cock."

It came as a bit of a shock the way Mitchell put it, but he was right, that's all I was: a tight ass for his thick cock. Maybe now I could answer my father's question as to what part I played. Although

Mitchell's description might have been hard to take, it was making me more aware of how tough one had to be to survive in this industry. It was a job like any other, except in most cases, you were just there to be used. I was pleased to know that I might earn some money the following day, but I was beginning to wonder if I'd made the right decision to go into the porno industry.

We thoroughly enjoyed our meal and after I'd helped Mitchell and Chris wash the dinner dishes, we went back to the lounge for coffee. I was beginning to view Mitchell as not only a friend, but as someone I could turn to in times of difficulty, and as for Chris, he was more a friend and confidante. I liked the two guys and I was happy for them that they had each other, and I hoped that one day I too might find someone to share my life with.

Our evening came to a close and although they offered to drive me home, I said I'd get a cab. Chris called a cab for me and soon I was heading back to the dreary side of town. As I neared my apartment, I saw the night guys plying their trade. I paid and got out of the cab, but instead of heading upstairs, I chose to stand in the street and watch the young guys at work. Cars were literally crawling passed them, heads turning and eyes following, like animals in search of their prey. A black car stopped next to a guy who looked no older than eighteen. I saw the young guy lean in through the passenger's window then withdraw his head. He looked up and down the street and then climbed into the car. Slowly the car moved off and I wondered what service he was going to offer and how much he'd earn.

As I stood there, a thin, young guy, who wasn't bad looking, approached me.

"Hi, mister. Do you have a light?"

"Sorry, I don't smoke," I said, sizing up the young man.

"You looking for something mister?"

I wasn't in need of sex, but I did wonder whether I should ask this young man how one went about becoming a hustler and what I had to do to earn extra money.

"You look like you've got something good hanging down your left leg there, mister."

I looked down and saw the outline of my cock etched against my denim jeans.

"Would you like to come upstairs for some coffee?" I asked the young man.

It was probably something out of the ordinary for him, because he seemed bemused by my offer, but he accepted. We made our way upstairs and I took him into my apartment.

As the coffee percolator set to work, he asked me what I wanted him to do. It was a simple question, but it was not what I expected. I stammered and stuttered.

"Would you like me to suck your dick for you, mister?"

My stammering and stuttering continued. I was hoping that I hadn't done the wrong thing by inviting him into my home. What if he had a gun or a knife?

"You look like you've got a good body and a good dick too, mister."

I looked at his face. It was weather-beaten yet handsome and when I thought of Chris and how young he looked, I wondered how old this 'boy' was.

The coffee was made and my guest gulped it down as though he hadn't eaten or drunk anything for days. I offered a second cup, but he refused. I watched as, when he'd finished his coffee how he ran his hand across the front of his tattered jeans. I could see how a bulge was beginning to develop, but I really didn't want to take him. I thought of asking him a number of questions, but something held me back. He moved closer to me and I wondered what his plan was, then he laid his hand on my crotch. To have his soft touch was erotic, and I immediately sprung a boner. His eyes lit up as he felt the length of my cock and before I could do anything, he'd ripped open my jeans, pulled out my hard cock and wrapped his mouth around it. I tried to push his head off it, but he clamped his lips tighter around my shaft and sucked frantically. It all seemed so clumsy but he at least knew how to bring a guy off quickly. Before I knew it, I shot a wad of warm cum into his mouth, which he promptly spat into his empty coffee cup, and then he took the next load and then spat that out. Once he had drained my cock of every last drop, he lifted his head from my throbbing cock and licked his lips.

"That'll be $50, mister."

Well, there I had my first price tag; for him a blow-job was worth $50. Maybe with my clean-cut looks, I could charge more.

I duly paid my young visitor, thanked him and let him out of the building, without him having his coffee, where he resumed his spot on the street, waiting for the next customer.

CHAPTER 7

THE BOSS JOINS IN

I was at the studio bright and early, and so was Mitchell.

"Who's the guy that we're filming with?" I asked Mitchell.

"Frank Holloway."

"What's he like?"

"Let me not spoil it for you; there he is," said Mitchell, pointing in the direction of Mr. Hamilton's office.

I looked in the direction pointed out to me and saw a guy of about six foot four heading our way. He had broad shoulders that tapered to a slim waist and his head was shaved and shone in the light. When I looked at him, I never got the idea that he might be a bottom. I looked at Mitchell and then back to the tall guy and tried to fathom out how Mitchell was the guy fucking him. This man looked like a giant.

Mitchell saw my expression and laughed.

"I know what's going through your mind, Chad!"

"What?" I teased.

"You're trying to work out how such a biog guy would allow himself to be fucked, and by me!"

I didn't deny it, but I remembered that Mitchell had said that by being versatile, you would have more work opportunities.

"Hi Frank, how's things?" asked Mitchell, grabbing the large man's hand and shaking it.

"Did you miss my ass yesterday?"

"Not really, I had this young ass instead," said Mitchell, pointing to me. "Let me introduce you. Frank this is Chad."

I smiled at him and felt his tight grip on my hand as we shook hands. I also tried to come to terms with the fact that this hulk of a man would have been screwed by Mitchell, had I not been there to take Frank's place in the movie. I looked the two of them and tried to conjure up in my mind what the scene would have been like. The more I 'conjured' the more I got a hard-on, until Mitchell passed a snide comment.

"I think something is beginning to show," he whispered to me.

I looked down and noticed a large bulge in the front of my jeans.

"Deep in thought were you; or deep inside someone?"

I smiled knowingly at Mitchell, who obviously was beginning to understand my warped mind.

The three of us made out way into the main building and headed to the studio in which Mitchell and I had worked the day before. The crew was all assembled and presently, Mr. Hamilton appeared, wearing what I considered an outfit not conducive to his role as business manager or director. Even Mitchell was a little taken aback by Mr. Hamilton's appearance.

"And this, Josh?" asked Mitchell.

"I decided that I would also be in the movie," replied Josh.

He had on a white string vest which revealed his dark skin beneath, and a pair of black leather jeans. Admittedly it looked appealing in a sexual nature and I actually thought he looked very sexy dressed like that. I had always had a passion for leather; both it's touch and smell and I could quite easily become aroused by the touch of the soft material on my skin. I had already experienced that when I'd done my strip show for Mrs. Hamilton.

"So what are we shooting today, boss?" requested Mitchell.

"It's going to be a 4-way shot," replied Mr. Hamilton.

I had visions of the boss getting into my ass again in an effort to short-change me financially.

"You're going to screw Chad, again, but this time I'm doing Frank and then half way through the scene, we're going to swap," said Mr. Hamilton, being very directorial.

"So when we swap," asked Mitchell, "are you going to get into Chad and I get into Frank?"

"No!" came the sharp reply. "I'm getting into you, Mitch," said Mr. Hamilton.

"But…"

"No buts my friend, I'm having your ass in this scene."

"But you know I'm not a bottom."

"The fans want it Mitch. They want to see you get fucked and today is the day."

I could see the word PANIC written across Mitchell's face. Maybe when he was very much younger, he might have played around with someone who might, just might have slipped their cock into him, but now it was a different thing as an adult. I took Mitchell to one side.

"Mitchell," I whispered so that Mr. Hamilton didn't hear me. "Why don't you say you've got something wrong with you, you know medical, and can't be penetrated?"

Mitchell stared at me bewilderedly.

"If you have to tell him you'd rather I'd do it because if I did, I'd be very gentle with you so that you weren't hurt, but if he does it to you, he's just going to ram that thick cock of his into you until you scream with pain. It'll give him a sense of power over you."

"I think I prefer plan B," said Mitchell into my ear. "But how are we going to do it?"

"Leave it to me and just go with me when I make my move on you. OK?"

Mitchell nodded and I could see a little less strain across his face.

"What are you two gossiping about?" asked Mr. Hamilton.

"Nothing sir. I was just giving Mitchell some advice on how to relax his ass when he's being penetrated."

"Right, let's get this thing rolling. We'll do an introduction to the scene later. Let's get straight to the action. Frank, I want you to lick over my crotch then unzip the leathers and take out my dick when you can feel it's hard. Suck it for a while then work my balls for me. When I think you've done enough, I'm going to do the same to you, but instead of stopping there, I'm going to rip your pants off and fuck you. Got it?"

"Yes Josh," answered a meek sounding Frank.

"You two guys, do exactly the same as us, then Mitch you bend him over and plow that fine ass of his. Ready?"

Everyone was ready; lights, camera crew and actors.

"Action!" shouted Mr. Hamilton.

Simultaneously, Frank started salivating over Mr. Hamilton's leather-covered crotch while Mitchell did the same to me. I was already hard when Mitchell started working on me and when the camera wasn't on us, we'd glance across at the other two. Mr. Hamilton's face was a picture of sublime peace as Frank brought the boss's dick to a higher state. Whenever the camera moved back to us, Mitchell and I would perform exceptionally well.

By the time Mitchell had my jeans around my ankles and had sunk his wonderful cock into me, Mr. Hamilton was pounding Frank's ass like an oil drill in search of the magic gold. Both men were wet with seat, while Mitchell and I looked surprisingly fresh. Mitchell and I watched, out of the corners of our eyes, the long, thick, dark dick slide effortlessly in and out of Frank's cavity while the giant of a man groaned and grunted with each thrust.

When Mr. Hamilton felt he was getting close, he shouted, "Change!" and he immediately withdrew from Frank and was heading in our direction, when Mitchell pulled out of me and I swiftly pulled on a condom, bent Mitchell over and aiming the stem of my cock, slowly pushed into Mitchell's tight ass. The cameras continued shooting as my cock slipped nicely into Mitchell's warm chute and we became connected. Mr. Hamilton stood watching, bewildered, stroking his hard cock and becoming frustrated.

"Cut!" he screamed. "What the fuck's going on here? I told you that ass was mine. I was the one to break that virgin ass in, not you, you little punk."

Everyone could feel his anger. There stood the naked boss, his heavy dick bobbing as he stomped up and down, ranting with anger and shouting at all who were within earshot. So angry was he that he stormed out of the studio without thinking to put his clothes back on. Mitchell, Frank and I looked at each other and then burst out laughing. Soon the crew saw the funny side to it and they joined in the laughter. Our laughter was soon broken up with the arrival of fatty who had come to collect Mr. Hamilton's clothes. He didn't know why we were laughing, but he'd been well trained to always take everything seriously, so all we saw of him was a scowling face and then he scuttle off his fat little body shuddering in all directions.

"Do you think I'll get fired?" I asked, still laughing.

"I don't know, but I wouldn't worry," replied Mitchell. "If he fires you, he'll also fire us, I suppose."

"Do you think the shoots over for the day?" inquired Frank, beginning to put his clothes back on.

"I would imagine so," said Mitchell, also getting dressed. "I think we might as well go home,; I doubt we'll get paid for today."

The three of us completed dressing and left the building, still talking about the episode.

"Would you like to come back to my place?" I asked both Frank and Mitchell, but both declined the invitation, which meant I had the rest of the day alone.

As Mitchell neared his car, I ran over to him and asked, "I hope I didn't hurt you?"

"Not at all but you've got yourself quite a sturdy weapon there Chad. That cock of yours could do some damage to some asses and I can tell you that anyone whose had a taste of that ass in them, will crave more of it."

"Does that mean you want more?" I joked.

He grinned at me, punched me gently on the arm and said, "You'll never know, kid."

CHAPTER 8

A MOMENT WITH MY DAD

Back at my apartment was a surprise waiting for me: my dad.

"Dad, what are you doing here?"

"I thought I'd take a chance and see if you were home."

"Well it's your lucky day because we're not shooting today so I was able to come home early. Come on in. How's Mum and Gran?"

"They're both well, thanks, and send their love."

We went into my apartment and I got my dad and me something to drink, then we sat in the lounge chatting. Naturally, my dad wanted to know how the work was getting on and still wanted to know the name of the film. I think he had visions of attending some world premiere and would then be able to brag to his friends that his son was a film star. A thought flashed through my mind; I wonder if he's already told all his buddies that his only son is in the movie industry and would soon have his name up in lights!

"So tell me, what are the people like that you work with, son?"

"Very nice, Dad."

"Any nice girls?"

I couldn't very well tell him that apart from the very first day when I went into the building, I saw a man screwing a woman; other than that there wasn't a woman to be seen.

"Not really, and in any case you don't have time to get to know them."

"But I assume you have met a few people that you have made friends with?"

"Oh yes, a couple of guys."

"And what do they do? Are they also actors like you?"

"Yeah, but you know they have lives of their own."

"Well I'm glad you're doing all right. The only thing I'm not too happy with is this area. You know when I was waiting for you and sitting in the car, some young chap came up to me and propositioned me."

"Oh, what did he want?"

"It's not what he wanted; it was what he was offering me."

I pretended to be innocent and naive.

"What was he offering you, Dad?"

I could see my dad get embarrassed, but I decided to press on.

"What was it, Dad?"

"He asked me if I wanted sex with him."

"Oh," I replied nonchalantly as though this was an everyday occurrence. "So did you take him up on his offer?"

"Don't be stupid, Chad. I'm not that way inclined."

"Did he offer you anything else?" I persisted.

"Well …"

"…yes?"

"Then he asked if I wanted just a blow-job or a hand job."

"So did you take either of those?"

"Of course not!"

"It worries me that there are those sorts of people hanging around where you are."

"Oh Dad, they're harmless and at least they're trying to make a living."

"Like that?"

"Well if you had the looks and you were down and out, what would you do?"

"Get a job."

"And if jobs are hard to come by, and you need to eat, then you must think of some way to make money."

My dad thought about what I had said, and then he looked at me earnestly and asked, "Do they pester you?"

"One or two have, but I don't take any notice of them."

"I hope you never get like that."

"Like what, Dad?"

"You know…"

"No, I don't know. I see them as normal human beings desperate to make ends meet. Obviously some of them have no homes to go to so they become a little weather-beaten if you want to put it that way, but perhaps, inside of them they have hearts of gold. Sometimes when I walk past them and see them, I say to myself, there by the grace of God, go I."

At that my dad looked shocked. He looked puzzled by the way I had reacted.

"You know, son, you've really grown up. To hear you talk with maturity makes me proud but also humbles me that you have to show your old man how to respect others."

I really loved my dad, and as much as I cared for him, I couldn't bring myself to tell him of my job and the thoughts that had run through my head about earning extra money, similar to what those young boys on the street were doing. There was an element of respect for him combined with an element of excitement that drove me to want to be like those boys, but I should not say 'like them', but rather 'do as they do'. I had a passion for sex, a passion for my body and above all, a passion for life, yet when I saw some of those boys; it appeared that life had left them. I didn't want an existence; I wanted the thrills that life had to offer.

My dad got up from where he was sitting and crossed over to the lounge window that overlooked the street below. He looked down and saw the group of young men loitering under streetlights and near store entrances, waiting – waiting for that magic moment of someone acknowledging their existence and they being able to offer that person something back in return.

I could see the expression of unhappiness on my dad's face, but I wondered exactly what was going through his mind.

"What's troubling you, Dad?"

He never turned to face me but remained silent and still. I moved over to the window and stood alongside him and also looked down at the young men below. We watched as a car or two would cruise slowly by and then stop while a young face would peer into the vehicle and then either the vehicle would drive off or the young man would get in and together with his trick, they'd leave the area.

"I think I'd better be going," he said softly without losing contact with the scene below.

"If you must Dad. I'm glad you popped round to see me."

It was then that he turned to me, took me in his arms and hugged me. My father had hugged me as a small boy, but never since I had grown up. I was taken by this and wondered what had brought it on, but I returned the feeling and wrapped my arms around him, pulling him closer to me. We stood there like two lovers, embracing each other, but I didn't know why he'd done it and I wasn't about to ask.

"I'll see you soon, son," he said, as he broke away from me.

I wasn't sure if it was a tear that I saw in his eyes or whether it was a trick of the light, but something had moved my dad and for the first time, I felt even closer to him.

"Please pop round whenever you feel like it, Dad."

"Thanks Chad, I will."

He opened the front door to my apartment and strode slowly out of the building. I watched from the lounge window as he got into his car and start the engine, and then he slowly drove past the young men who all stared at him as he drove by, and then he disappeared around a corner. I remained watching the young men for a long time, thinking of my dad as I did so.

The stillness of the moment was suddenly shattered by the incessant ringing of the telephone. It brought me back rapidly to reality and I rushed to pick up the receiver.

"Hello, Chad speaking."

"Chad, it's Mr. Hamilton here. I looked for you and the others after the shoot today, but you all seemed to have disappeared."

"Yes, sir, we left together."

"Are the others there with you?"

"No sir. I don't know where they are."

"Are you alone?"

I didn't want to see him as I wasn't sure what his intentions were and I'd just had a 'heavy' moment with my dad, so answered and said that I wasn't.

"I'm sorry sir, but my Dad's visiting at the moment."

"Oh, in that case I won't bother you. I'd like to see you at the office tomorrow, if that's OK with you."

"Sure, sir. I'll see you then."

I replaced the receiver and wondered what his motive was for phoning.

CHAPTER 9

A TIME TO RETHINK

The following morning, I made my way to the studio, oblivious of what was in store for me. It didn't take me long to reach the buildings and when I went in fatty was there to meet me. I told him that I had a meeting with Mr. Hamilton, but he informed me that the boss had not arrived yet.

"Are they filming today?" I asked, wondering if the meeting was to discuss a scene we might be shooting.

Fatty merely glared at me as though I had asked some very personal question. I decided to find the answer for myself, so I left fatty's office on the pretext that I needed the bathroom, and headed in the direction of the studio in which we shot most of our scenes.

As I entered I saw a couple of guys, who I had never seen before, preparing themselves for their shoot. As I never recognized anyone there, I assumed it must be a different film that was being made, so I returned to fatty's office. By the time I got back, Mr. Hamilton had arrived.

"Mr. Hamilton will see you now," said the discontented fat man.

I made my way through the office and entered Mr. Hamilton's office. He was seated behind his huge desk, busy reading a letter.

"Morning sir."

"Morning Chad. Have a seat."

I sat down and waited for him to finish reading. When he had done so, he signed the letter, laid it down and looked up at me.

"I gave yesterday's incident a great deal of thought, and I've made a decision."

I looked at him in anticipation. He had no smile, nor did he look as though he was going to make a pass at me.

"You undermined my authority. I told you that you were to swap partners and I was to take Mitch while you were to go with Frank, but you deliberately disobeyed me."

"No sir…"

"I haven't finished!"

There was a moment of silence.

"When I say something, people listen and you didn't. You made your own decision and in this business, the director makes the decisions, not the actors. You need us; we don't need you."

This I thought a little immature because without the actors, they wouldn't have any films, but this was his view.

"I can't have people working for me who undermine my authority and in the process, undermine the making of my films. Therefore, I'm asking you to leave. Your services will no longer be needed."

It felt as though an arrow had been fired and I'd been hit between the eyes. The shock was intense. I thought I might get a rapping over the hand, but not actually be fired. I looked somewhat dumbfounded by his remark and sat staring at him. I wasn't sure whether to cry or not.

"If you have any personal things on the property, I want you to remove them and I want you out of the building in fifteen minutes otherwise I'll have you thrown out by security."

What security, I thought. The only security that Mr. Hamilton had was fatty in the next door office.

"Sure sir," I said, as proudly as I could manage.

I stood up, smiled at him and turned to go.

"Chad! You're a good looking young man and I'm sure you'll do well for yourself, but you need to learn about this industry."

I never responded, but walked calmly out of the building and into the bright sunlight. As I made my way out of the grounds, I saw Mitchell arrive. I didn't know whether I should say anything to him, and was about to pretend I hadn't seen him, when I heard him call me.

"Hey Chad. Where are you off to?"

I merely looked at him, tears beginning to well up in my eyes.

"Home," was the pathetic reply.

"Hey! What's going on?" he asked coming up to me quickly.

"I've been fired."

"What? Because of what happened with us?"

I nodded my head.

"Shit! The bastard! But you did it for me."

"It doesn't matter Mitchell."

I didn't know what else to say to him, but the longer he stayed talking to me, the more the tears were streaming down my face. I gave him one last look and headed home as quickly as I could. When I got home to my apartment, I just threw myself onto my bed and cried; maybe it was out of self-pity, I wasn't sure.

I must have cried myself to sleep because it was the incessant ringing of my telephone that awoke me. By the time that I had realized what the noise was and got up to answer it, it had cut off. The sun was still blazing down on the street below and the traffic was cruising up and down with a few young boys doing what I affectionately called the 'lunchtime' shift. As I looked down, I noticed my young friend who gave me the blow-job standing, leaning up against a wall. I immediately grabbed my apartment keys and headed downstairs and out into the street. As I approached him, he recognized me.

"Hi mister, you looking for some fun?"

"Not really, but you never had your coffee when I last saw you. Would you like to come up and have it now?"

I realized that by spending time with me, he would be losing potential income, so I volunteered to give him $50 for me to talk to him.

"That's a weird offer, mister, but OK; only half an hour though."

I thought he drove a hard bargain, but what the hell.

We made our way back upstairs and I made the coffee that I had promised. He sat himself down in the lounge and waited for his coffee. For some reason, I didn't feel so threatened this time. I left him in the lounge while I prepared the coffee and was soon sitting back with him.

"Why are you paying me $50 to talk to me?" enquired my quizzical friend.

"First tell me your name; your real name."

"You mean the name my mother gave me?"

"Yes."

"It's Harry, but I think that's a shit name, so I go by the name of Hank. And your name?"

"Mine's Chad, and that's my real name."

"Hank I know you've seen me around just as I've seen you around, but I don't think you know what I do."

"You're not a cop are you?"

I laughed.

"No, nothing like that. I've been working for that film studio round the corner from here.

"Hey are you one of those porn stars?"

I immediately envisioned him thinking I would be rolling in money and that I had my name up in lights; therefore he could try and rip me off.

"No, Hank, I'm not a porn star. Sure I was making a movie, but things changed today and I was fired."

"That's a bummer," he replied, sipping his coffee. "Why?"

"Why was I fired?"

"Yeah."

"It's a bit of a long story and as I only have half an hour with you, I'll cut it short. I fucked the star and the boss wanted to do that."

He roared with laughter.

"What's the joke?"

"Was it that Mr. Hamilton dude?"

"Yes, do you know him?"

"We all know him. He's as mean as shit. He likes to fuck us guys, but doesn't want to pay."

Hearing Hank's story made me feel a lot better.

"Pity you didn't fuck him silly," continued Hank, still chuckling at the knowledge that someone had got the better of Mr. Hamilton. "But what's that got to do with me?"

"Before I started in movies, I used to be a stripper, but now that I've been fired, I'll have to make money somehow and I was wondering…"

"…you wanna be a hustler like us?"

I paused and then nodded.

"You know what it involves?"

"I think so, but I'm not sure how you go about it, other than waiting to be picked up."

"Listen, you've got to be careful. You look a decent sort of guy and I don't think you'll fit in, if you know what I mean."

I didn't actually, but I let him carry on.

"We get all types of guys. There are some who are out to fuck us up because they feel like it; then you get those who aren't getting it from their wives, like Mr. Hamilton: they're not too bad, but the worst are the kinky ones."

"You mean the ones that beat you up?"

"So you know then? Yeah those are the bastards. They want a bit of your ass, but then they get carried away and tie you up or beat you up. The more pain they put you through, the better they enjoy themselves. I don't like them," he said, sadness appearing in his face. "You see, the problem is that when they pick you up, you've got no idea what sort of person they are. It's only once they've got you in some isolated place or hotel room that their fun begins."

"Have you ever thought of giving it all up, Hank?"

Again he roared with laughter.

"You ask me that and you're the one who wants to join up!"

"I'm only thinking of a way to make some money," I replied.

"The other thing is the pimp."

"What do you mean?"

"Us guys down there; we've got our pimp and he looks out for us and sometimes tells us where we have to go."

"What's he like?"

"Hey, I suppose there's times when he's Ok, but other times he's a brute."

"Would I have to have a pimp?"

"No, but you'll soon see one appear, especially if you're on his turf."

"So this street downstairs, is that your pimp's turf?"

"Sort of, I suppose. It's just that I've never seen any other pimps around there."

Hank finished his coffee, looked at the lounge clock on the wall and said, "half hour's up, Chad. Pity I couldn't have given you head or something as well; you've got an awesome cock. It's one of the best I've tasted."

I don't know if Hank was flattering me in an effort to squeeze more money from me, but I was now unemployed so I couldn't accommodate him.

"You wouldn't like me to give you a blow-job for $50?" I offered.

Hank looked shocked.

"Hey, I've got to earn money too and you could be my first customer," I remarked.

To my astonishment, Hank stood up, unzipped his jeans, pulled a good length of boy cock and said, "Go for it, but for free."

I looked at what was offer and liked what I saw, so I sank onto his cock and gave him a good, slow blow-job until I felt his balls rise in his sac and felt the first blast of warm cum hit my throat.

When I had sucked the last drops from Hank's cock, he zipped up, smiled at me and thanked me for the service.

"You could make it big in this business, Chad, but be careful if you do."

With that, young Hank went back to his chores on the street below and I started to think of a possible new career.

CHAPTER 10

NIGHT OUT

I dialed Greg's number, on the off chance he might be at home. It was two months since I had last spoken to him, so I thought I'd give him a call. Fortunately he answered.

"Hi there, Greg speaking."

"Hi Greg, it's Chad. How are things with you and married life?"

"Still going strong, but how are you? I haven't heard from you for ages. Where are you because I tried your number and was told you weren't there?"

"Was it my Gran that told you that?"

"I really don't know, but it did sound like an elderly person, so where are you?"

"Greg, it's a long story but I moved out of home and got my own apartment."

"Where? And what are you doing?"

"It's on the other side of town and I'm doing nothing at the moment."

"Are you still doing nothing?"

"I did a stint of filming, but that's fallen through."

"Filming! You mean you're a film star?"

"Nothing as grand as that," I said, and then lowered my voice. "It was a porno movie."

A shriek of laughter came swiftly down the line.

"You're joking!"

"I'm serious."

"Maybe I can believe that because you got all the assets a porn star needs."

"Thanks for the vote of confidence."

"What's the movie called, because I have to get it when it comes out."

"You're not going to believe this, but I don't know. I got booted out before they'd finished filming."

"Why?"

"I shagged the guy that the director was hoping to shag."

Again there were peals of laughter.

"Trust you, you can't keep that delicious cock of your away from any hole, can you? So what are you doing?"

"Nothing, that's why I phoned you. I wondered if you knew anyone who might want a stripper for a night. I really need to earn some money."

"Well, you know you can strip for me any time."

"I know that, but I wondered if you knew anyone who would pay."

"I might pay you."

"I'm serious Greg."

"So am I. But tell me, what's you address then I can pop around and see you, if you're free at any time."

I gave Greg my address and then asked how Fred was.

"I still think of that night when the three of us got together, that was fun," I remarked

"Funny you should mention that, because it was only the other day that Fred mentioned it to me. You're right it was great. Maybe we should do it again."

"Listen Chad, I can't chat too long as we were on our way out, but I will keep in touch, now that I have your phone number and address. Take car my friend."

As I replaced the receiver, I was glad that I had spoken to Greg. It' s good to keep in touch with friends.

The rest of the day passed by uneventfully and I was surprised that Mitchell hadn't phoned because I was sure he'd have got all the details from the studio. As the evening settled down, I had a shower and pulled on a pair of jeans and a skimpy T-shirt. I then made my way downstairs and stood in the entrance to the apartment block, looking out at the boys doing the 'night shift' on the street. Hank was there, so I walked slowly towards him, keeping my eyes on the street to look out for passing cars.

"Hi Hank."

"Chad, what are you doing here?"

"I thought I'd give it a try. I'd like to stick with you, if you don't mind so that I can learn. Do you mind?"

Although Hank might have thought I was competition for him, I had said that if someone did pick me up, the agreement was that both hank and I would go with the guy. Once Hank heard this, he was more willing to take me under his wing.

"How old are you, Hank?"

"Eighteen, and you?"

"Nineteen, but I'll be turning twenty, one of these days."

"I thought you were a bit older, but I don't mean that in a shit way."

"I know what you mean. Quite a few guys think I'm in my twenty's. Tell me, what must I do?"

"Just stick by me, but if our pimp comes by, pretend you're a trick wanting me for some fun, otherwise he's gonna drive you off his turf."

I understood my position and while we continued our idle chat, I kept an eye open for passing cars. A couple of cars drove slowly past and one even came to a stop while its driver surveyed what was on offer. At about 8:00 p.m, a car stopped in front of Hank and me and the passenger window was rolled down. A blond haired guy of about thirty- something leaned across to us and beckoned us. As we both advanced, he indicated that he didn't want Hank, but me. I continued to the car and leaned in.

"What are you looking for?" I asked, trying to sound like a real pro.

"Nice crotch and ass," said the blond. "How much to fuck my ass?"

I didn't know what the going price was as I'd forgotten to ask Hank, so I did the next best thing.

"How much you got?"

I know it probably made me sound desperate, but I didn't know what else to say.

"$200."

To me $200 was a lot of money but then I might have been under charging, so I resorted to plan B.

"Let me get a smoke and think about it," I said, turning and heading to Hank.

"What's up?" asked Hank.

"He wants me to fuck him for $200. Is that too little," I whispered.

"Fuck yes. Tell him you'll suck him off for that."

"But you only charged me $50 for a blow-job."

"That's 'cause I liked you and I knew you wanted it."

I turned around, without the cigarette and wandered casually back to the car.

"I've thought about it and I'll give you a blow-job for your $200."

He looked me up and down and then shrugged his shoulders and drove off.

"Oh well, it's his loss. He doesn't know how good my mouth is," I said, heading back to Hank.

"I've never seen him before," said Hank, "but he wasn't bad looking."

A few more cars passed by and then a regular of Hank's stopped and the young boy ran over to the passenger's window. They chatted for a while, then he turned to me, called me and I made my way to the car.

"Joe, this is my friend Chad. How about the two of us for $400? He's got an awesome cock, I can promise you; I've seen it and you'll enjoy it."

Joe looked at both of then he said we could get in. Hank hopped in the front and I climbed in the back and off we sped. Joe looked to be middle-aged with a slight paunch and some receding hair, but other than that he wasn't unpleasant to look at. We drove a short way and then stopped outside a small apartment block, where we all got out and Joe led us upstairs to his dingy apartment. I say 'dingy' only because it was pretty dark when we entered, but once he'd pout on the lights, it looked a little better. There was no hanging about. Joe led Hank and me straight to his bedroom which had a double bed, a side table on which stood a large container of lube, and a pile of condoms which lay scattered on the table top and nothing else, and then he stripped off his clothes and lay on the bed, naked. I looked at Hank and he indicated that we strip.

Hank got undressed before I did, so he climbed straight onto the bed and began sucking Joe's fat cock. Once I was naked, I saw how Joe pushed Hank out of the way so that he take a look at me.

"Fuck, you were right about the guy's dick, it's a monster."

"I told you, you wouldn't be disappointed," said Hank indicating me to join him on the bed.

Hank was busy lathering up Joe's uncut cock so I took my lead from him and together we licked and sucked along the length of Joe's cock, while he lay watching us and running his fingers through our hair.

"Bring me that monster cock," he instructed me, so I released my attention on his cock, slid up the bed and positioned myself above his face so that he could take my shaft down his throat.

He slurped my delicious cock, as Greg had called it, pulling it deep into his throat while I pumped in and out of his mouth. His sound effects as he sucked on my cock were almost humorous; they sounded like a vacuum cleaner that was blocked and then cleared of its obstruction. His breathing was heavy and I wondered if he was about to shoot his load, but he wasn't.

We soon found ourselves in different positions, with Hank lying on his back and Joe now kneeling between Hank's legs, attacking my young friend's balls and asshole while I did likewise to Joe. Once more as my tongue worked wonders in his ass, so the sound effects erupted again, except this time it included expletives such as "Fuck me big boy" and "ram that dick into my hole" and "fuck the shit out of me, fucker!" As we were being paid for this, I thought I'd better oblige.

I could see that Hank was dying to have Joe penetrate him, so before I made my entrance, I gave Joe and instruction.

"Get that dick of yours into Hank. Slide it in ever so gently so he can enjoy the feel."

Joe was obviously a good student, if one could call him that, because he obeyed and slowly pushed his cock deep into Hank, who smiled broader the deeper Joe sank. Once Joe was completely embedded in Hank's ass, I aimed my hard cock at his throbbing pucker and drove in. I heard Joe's cries as my thick cock stretched his opening and once it had broken through his tight sphincter and slid into his chute, Joe's cries changed to whimpers of joy. Joe and I built up a simultaneous rhythm with him sliding into Hanks and me plowing into him.

The three of us maintained our positions until we all shot our load and then we collapsed on each other in a cum-soaked bundle on the bed.

"You were right, Hank, your friend certainly knows how to use that weapon of his. That was worth every cent."

After we'd cleaned ourselves and Joe had paid Hank, who immediately gave me half, Joe took us back to the street corner where he'd picked us up.

As we neared the spot, Hank suddenly called out, "Stop! Drop us here Joe."

I was startled and wondered why he'd said this as we weren't exactly back at the street; we probably had another fifty to seventy-five yards to go.

"Sure, replied Joe, "but why?"

"Just drop us here, Joe, and thanks for the great time," continued Hank, hastily emerging from the car.

I followed suit and watched as Hank pretended to hide in some shadows.

"Why are you hiding?" I whispered to Hank.

Joe had dropped us and driven on, probably back home.

"Chad, make your way to your apartment and pretend you don't know me."

"But why, Hank?"

"It's my pimp. If he sees you he's bound to ask questions and I don't want you involved."

I did as I was told and casually walked along the street as though I'd just appeared from another part of town, which I had, and was on my way home. Hank, on the other hand, sauntered along as though he was waiting for someone to pick him up, stopping on occasions to look into a store window. The other young boys continued either chatting to driver's who stopped or chatting to each other.

"I haven't seen you tonight, Hank?" I heard a gruff voice say. "You been busy?"

"Not so busy, replied Hank, nonchalantly, "just gave a guy head, that's all. It's quiet tonight."

As I walked past some of the boys, they smiled knowingly at me but never said anything. I saw how their pimp, who looked a brute of a man, glanced my way, but I kept walking into my apartment building and ignored them.

I got up to my apartment, went in without putting on the lounge light, and looked out of the window. I saw Hank talking to one of his mates, probably telling him of our escapade but I didn't see the pimp. I then went into the bathroom, turned on the shower tap and stood naked under it, letting the cool water run over my tired body. I stood under the shower of water, thinking about the night's events and found myself grinning at nothing in particular except the joy of having made $200 for a night out.

I climbed out of the shower, still with all the apartment lights out and wandered back to the lounge window where I dried myself while I watched the action on the street. I looked for Hank and saw him chatting to a driver, who had just pulled up, then I saw him get into the car and away they drove. That's when a realization came to me: although they made quite a bit of money on any night, what was their health like. I wondered how many times a night Hank was being screwed by some guy somewhere in the city. No wonder some of the boys looked so weather-beaten. Is this what I wanted? Not if I could help it. Maybe I could become a selective hustler; one who did it by invitation only and to high-class clients, but how was I going to attract those high-class people?

Once I had dried myself, I padded through to my bedroom and threw myself onto my bed, closed my eyes and fell asleep pretty soon.

I don't know what time it was, but I was woken by knocking on my front door. Still half asleep, I wander through and peeped through the peep-hole in the door. I saw Hank standing there. I opened the door and let him in.

"Are you busy with someone?" he asked, seeing me naked.

"No, I was sleeping. What are you doing here?"

"It was late and I couldn't get home so I was wondering if I could spend the night here with you?"

I was too tired to argue, so I said that he could. I made my way back to my room and the last thing I said to him was find a place to sleep. I hadn't been in bed for more than a minute when I felt the bed give as Hank slid in next to me. I felt his thin arms circle my waist and felt him cuddle up close to my body and I know I felt good.

At first I couldn't get back to sleep as I wasn't used to sharing a bed with someone all night, but I must admit, it was a fine feeling having him there; so fine in fact that I found myself getting a hard-on, but so was Hank.

"No funny business; I want to sleep," I said as I felt his thin fingers curl around the shaft of my swollen cock.

"Sure," he replied, without letting go of his hold. "This is how I usually sleep," he added.

"Liar," I answered, but never moved his hand away.

It must have been about seven in the morning when my doorbell rang and I wandered out to the lounge, but this time I had a towel wrapped around my waist. I opened the door.

"Dad! What are you doing here so early?"

"Just popped in before I went to work to see how you were."

I stood staring at my dad, not knowing what to say because Hank was still fast asleep in my bed.

"Am I going to get offered some coffee?"

"Oh yes…yes, I'm sorry Dad. Come into the kitchen and talk to me there."

My dad followed me and I put on the coffee percolator.

"Mum and Gran send their love as usual and want to know why they haven't been invited round to see your place."

"Dad, you know what Mum's like; she'd start saying this isn't right and that's in the wrong place and she'd start ruling my life for me."

"Oh, son, she's not that bad," he replied laughing as he said it. "So aren't you going to work this morning, or what time do you start?"

"We're not shooting today, Dad."

"That's nice, then maybe we could go out somewhere together."

"But you've got work to go to, haven't you?"

"I'm sure I could be like the others at work and call in sick."

Again he laughed at his own suggestion, but I didn't. I wasn't about to go out with my dad and leave Hank in my apartment alone. I didn't know him that well to leave my things in his care.

Just as I was thinking of some feeble excuse, I heard the toilet flush. Oh shit! Hank was awake and I was sure he'd come through to the kitchen looking for me, and he might even come through naked!

"You got someone here, son?"

"Uhm… yes, Dad."

"Hey, I'm sorry. I didn't want to upset your routine, so maybe I won't call in sick and get to work."

I felt awful that it was like I was chasing my dad away, but I'd rather do that than try to explain who Hank was and why he was here.

"Is she pretty?" asked my dad, nudging me.

I just gave one of my 'stupid' looks which he understood.

"Then let me be going. I'm sorry we can't spend time together, but maybe another day, hey?"

"That would be great Dad."

I showed him to the door and had just closed it when I heard a voice behind me, "who was that?"

There stood Hank with a vertical hard-on, looking very satisfied with himself.

"How about coming back to bed seeing that you don't have a job," he said, and took me by the hand and led me to my bedroom.

CHAPTER 11

SUCCESS

It had been about a week or two and I hadn't heard or seen Mitchell since I had been fired, so when I received a call from Chris, his partner, I was quite surprised.

"Chad, Mitch and I were wondering if we might pop round and see you tonight."

"That sounds great. I'd like that because I haven't seen you guys for so long."

"What time would suit you?" enquired Chris.

"I'm not gong out or doing anything, so why don't you drop in for a bite to eat. Say 7:00pm, if that's OK with you?"

"That's fine because I'm filming in the morning and I'll be free from lunch time and I'm sure Mitch's free from about 4:00pm."

"Then I'll see you two tonight. Looking forward to that," I said and then replaced the receiver.

I thought it a little strange that Chris had phoned after I'd been out of work for some time now and Mitch hadn't made contact with me. I wasn't sure why Mitch had done that, after all, I felt that I'd defended him and although I didn't expect any sort of pay-back, the least I thought I deserved was a call from him. Any rate, I don't hold grudges and was glad that they had eventually made contact with me.

At precisely 7:00, the doorbell rang and Chris and Mitchell arrived. I was genuinely pleased to see them and they both looked extremely well.

"Come in, come in," I said, leading the way into the lounge. "Drinks? What'll you have?"

"Beer for me," said Mitchell, and Chris asked for a martini.

"How have you guys been?" I shouted from the kitchen as I collected the drinks.

"Fine," shouted Mitchell, "but more importantly, how have you been?"

I walked out of the kitchen and into the lounge with our drinks. I placed them on the coffee table and sat down in an easy chair opposite my two friends.

"I'm surviving, I suppose."

"What have you been doing with yourself?" asked Chris. "Mitch told me what happened."

"I've tried to keep myself busy," I answered.

"Have you got a job?" asked Mitchell.

I was loathe to tell them of my escapades into a watered down version of being a hustler in case they saw it in the wrong light, so I opted for the easy way out.

"Not yet," I answered without elaborating.

"Well, we might have something for you," replied Mitchell.

I know I must have looked surprised, because they both grinned at me.

"I'm sorry that we weren't in contact with you, Chad, but I wanted to try and do something for you seeing that you'd done me a favor. After you were fired, I spoke to Chris and he spoke to his film company; you know the one that specializes in making twink and teen movies, well things might be about to happen."

I'm sure my face was a picture of joy. Chris took over the story.

"I spoke to the director and told him I knew someone who would fit into the type of movies we made and in particular a new movie we're making called *'Jason and the Argonauts'*," said Chris. "The director was looking for a guy who looked a little older than the other actors but wasn't in the 'older' category."

"So, I'm 'older' am I?" questioned Mitchell.

"Of course you're not," retorted Chris, giving his partner a tender kiss on the cheek as he said it.

"So where do I fit in?" I asked.

"He wants to meet you with the possibility of you playing the part of Jason."

"That sounds brilliant," I responded. "When can I meet him?"

"Well that's why we needed to see you tonight. You have an appointment with him tomorrow at 9:00a.m, but Mitch will pick you up at 8:00a.m and bring you to our place, then you and I can go to the studio together."

I became like a little kid with excitement. I knew I didn't have the job yet, but to be considered was a step in the right direction.

"Have you any idea what it's about, Chris?"

"I don't know exactly, but I think it's about this guy, Jason, who goes in search of some guys, but I'm sure the director will tell you more."

I leapt up and hugged both Mitchell and Chris and thanked them profusely. Once we had got over the excitement, I asked Mitchell how things were at the studio with Mr. Hamilton.

"He's still being himself, but he hasn't tried to get into my ass again. I'm not sure whether he realized that he was treading on dangerous ground or not, but he's kept well away from me."

"After what Mitch told me about the whole event, I laughed so much because I just imagined how angry he would have been. You know he always has to get his own way and if he doesn't, he doesn't know how to handle the situation except try and get the person concerned out of his life; but don't you worry, it'll probably come back to haunt him at some later stage," said Chris, with a smirk on his face.

"I'm not a vindictive person, Chris, but you know I couldn't even explain why I did it; he wouldn't let me."

"Trust me, you're better off without him, Chad," said Mitchell, offering his support.

"Listen guys, I wasn't going to ruin your appetites with my bad cooking skills, so we're having Chinese take-away for dinner, if that's OK with you."

"That's fine for both of us," said Mitchell, "in fact, that's our favorite take-away."

"I think it's everyone's. Come on, let's get the dishes from the kitchen and if you need a top up to drink, you can help yourselves."

As we rose to go to the kitchen, Chris looked out of the lounge window to the street below.

"Chad, do these guys ever get much trade down there?"

"You'd be surprised how much traffic flows up and down this street, even during the day," I answered. "I think I can tell you guys …"

"…what?" asked Mitchell.

"I tried it the other night."

"You tried what?" asked Chris.

"I went with one of the boys down there. A regular of his pitched up and we went with the guy."

Both Mitchell and Chris stood gob-smacked.

"You mean…" stammered Chris, with a grin on his face.

"Yes, the two of us went off with the guy, we had sex, got paid and then I came home."

Mitchell and Chris burst out laughing.

"How much did you score?" asked Mitchell.

"$200 each."

"For what?

"I had to screw the guy while he did it to the young boy."

"So you're a quiet hustler, are you?" teased Mitchell.

"Yep! From now on you pay for me."

All three of us laughed and laughed as we settled down to our Chinese take-away.

It was so good to have their company for the evening and we laughed and joked, ate and drank, until it was time for Mitchell and Chris to leave. I reminded Chris that I'd see him the following morning and gave them a last minute warning not to mess around with the guys on the street or they would have me to deal with!

The following morning I was up bright and early; showered, dressed and ready for my meeting at the studio where Chris worked. As promised, Mitchell arrived on the dot of 8:00 and took me back to his place where Chris was waiting. I was obviously a little nervous about the meeting, but Chris put me at ease and on the way to the studio, told me what to expect.

"If he asks whether you've had film experience, say no. Don't tell him anything about the problem with Mr. Hamilton. They don't like to hear stories of trouble actors may have had. Other than that, just be honest. You can tell him about the stripping and he'll probably ask you to strip for him, but you won't have a problem with that. Let your body talk for you, after all you don't really have to act in these movies, and from what Mitch has told me about you, I think you're in the running for the part."

"Do you know whether there'll be any other hopefuls there?"

"That I'm not sure of, but don't worry about them, if there are some. Even if you don't get this part, at least he will have seen you and he might put you on his books for future use. The important thing is to get known and then get exposure. Oh, and another thing, if you do get the job, whatever events are held, go to them. If parties are arranged, go to them as well. In fact, go to everything you are invited to so that people can see you and get to know you. I know sometimes it might be boring or the people there don't interest you – just go."

"Thanks for all the tips, Chris; it's really very kind of you and Mitchell to do this for me."

"It's our pleasure."

We arrived at the studio lot, which appeared larger than Mr. Hamilton's, and Chris directed me to the reception where I was introduced to a very sweet young guy and told him who I was and that I had a meeting with the director, Mr. Tomlinson. I sat in the foyer for a while, as it wasn't quite 9:00a.m yet, but on the stroke of 9:00a.m, a call came through and I was told to report to the director's office. The young receptionist led me along a long, narrow corridor until we reached the end and we were confronted by double glass doors.

"Just knock and wait to be called in," said the young man, who scuttled back to his reception desk.

I knocked twice, gently and waited.

"Come in," boomed a voice from behind the glass doors.

I entered and closed the doors behind me. I was in a large, spacious office with an equally large desk behind which sat a man. Opposite him at the desk were two chairs and against one of the walls stood a three-seater couch.

"You must be Chad," said the man behind the desk, looking up at me.

He looked as if he was about mid-thirties in age, had broad shoulders, a mop of dark brown hair and soft facial features.

He stood up to shake my hand across the desk, and then offered me a seat opposite him.

"I'm Brad Tomlinson, the director of *Virilis Films.* Please call me Brad."

The fact that he seemed so casual made me feel more at ease. I sat down and admired the man's pleasing features.

"Chris spoke to me about you when I mentioned that I was looking for a new face for my up-coming film, but tell me something about yourself, Chad."

"Well, I'm twenty, I'm unemployed at the moment and I think I've got what's needed for your type of films."

"I take it you know what type of films we make here?"

"Oh yes; that's why I think I have what it takes."

"Tell me, do you have any objections to being naked or having scenes that include nudity?"

"Not at all, Brad. To earn a little income, I've been stripping at parties around town."

"Oh so you have no problems of people seeing you naked?"

"Not at all."

"That's good, because so many young boys come here and when they get into the studio and see all the crew around them, they panic, but if you're used to being naked in front of people, well, then that's an asset."

"I really have no problem at all, Brad. In fact I'm proud of my body so I have no reason to show embarrassment."

"Fine. I'm sorry to ask all these questions which might seem a little personal, but I need to know that the people I hire have no hang-ups."

"Not at all. You can ask away."

"Chad, do you consider yourself a top or a bottom?"

"I don't have a problem being either, but I do prefer being a top."

"Great, we don't have enough of them. Are there any sexual acts that you wouldn't do?"

"It's not that I wouldn't necessarily do these, but I haven't experienced them before, but I don't think I'd do anything that involved scenes of someone pissing or crapping on me."

"We don't include scenes like those, Chad, so you have nothing to worry about. What I was thinking of involved such things as bondage or leather."

"Oh sorry. I don't have a problem with either. In fact I find leather quite a turn-on."

"Well, I'm very glad to hear that. Now could I ask you to please stand up?"

I did as was requested and so did Brad. He moved around his desk to my side and stood next to me. As I stood there, he walked casually around me, surveying every aspect of my body, clothed.

"Please take off your shirt, Chad."

I did so and again Brad wandered around me.

"Very impressive body you have there. Do you work out?"

"Not really," I responded.

"And now could we drop the jeans, but keep your briefs on."

I unzipped my jeans, kicked off my shoes and stepped out of my denims and stood in my white briefs.

Again Brad did his walk-about, and then I felt his hand on my ass. Instinctively I tensed.

"Just relax Chad."

I did so.

"Hm! That feels good. It's firm and nicely rounded. Could we drop the briefs please?"

I pulled them down to my ankles, allowing my package freedom. I put my hand under my balls and lifted them and stroked my cock once, then Brad began to inspect. He looked down at my cock and then up to my face and smiled.

"Are you sure, you're only twenty?"

I nodded and smiled back.

"You're a very big boy then. I really like what I see and what I see I can use. Thank you Chad, you can get dressed now."

Throughout this whole procedure, I was impressed how polite Brad had been and that there'd never been any lasciviousness on his part. I pulled on my clothes as he made his way back to behind his desk, where he collected some papers. Once I was dressed, he suggested we sit on the couch and casually discuss the film and my future.

I sat down next to Brad and noticed for the first time his muscularly formed thighs and long legs.

"I'll come straight to the point, Chad, I'd like to offer a job in my company and I would like to offer you a part in my next film."

"Thank you sir, I really appreciate that."

"The movie I'm about to make is called *Jason and the Argonauts* and I would like you to take the part of Jason."

"Thank you, I'd be very honored to have that part, but can you tell me something of the plot."

"Sure. As Jason, you're on a quest to find the ideal man, which takes you to the four quarters of the earth as you search for that dream man, and then you eventually find him and live happily ever after. That's the basic plot. Of course there are some sub-plots running along, but I won't go into all the details just yet, suffice to say you will get a lot of ass to deal with," said Brad, with a wry smile.

"I certainly don't have a problem with that, Brad."

"I'm very glad to hear that. Now, I'm going to ask my secretary to draw up a contract for you and once that's been done, I'd like you to come in and sign it, but today, I'd like you to spend some time here having a look around the studios. I'm sure we can get Chris to take you around and if not, I'll find someone else."

Brad stood up and extended a hand to me. I took his firm grip and shook his hand. I felt that I was back on the road to success.

CHAPTER 12

AT LAST A PART

My contract had been duly signed by both Brad and me and the agreement was that I would be paid $2000 for the making of the film *Jason and the Argonauts*. I was happy and so was Chris as he'd been cast as one of the Argonauts. Very basically the story was supposed to be about poor me (Jason) in a desperate search for a man. Now where have we heard that before? Well, any rate, Jason set off on a quest around the world in search of his perfect man – where have we heard that as well, and along the way, he meets up with a variety of men who have to be vetted to see if they fit the category and in the end … but if I tell you the ending, you're not going to buy the movie. Some of the Argonauts get a once over, while others do not even get a look in while a few get more than a once over! Filming was going to start in a week's time to allow the props department to come up with various scenes and the costume department could find the necessary costumes. You might laugh at the idea of the actors wearing costumes in a porn movie with so much nudity, but we have to start somewhere.

The story starts in Greece in the ancient times and those of us in the opening scene get to wear little skirt-like costumes with sandals and very little else. Brad had also made the decision to include some of the crew who were older men to play the parts of senators or elders, but they would not be in any of the sex scenes – for obvious reasons. Chris had been cast as a young boy living in ancient Mesopotamia and was to play a guy in the army. He was lucky to have as his costume a rather more ornate skirt-like outfit with a couple of leather harnesses across his chest to suggest his manliness. There were some young boys who represented Romans while others, the African-American guys among the group, were cast as Egyptians. It must be made clear that when I say Jason traveled the world in search of his ideal man, the world during that period was relatively small.

The opening scene was to be a market place in Greece where a number of young boys would be playing while a few adults went about their trading. One of the young boys meets up with his friend and they hide within one of the shop trading stores where they have sex together. While they are busy, Jason spies on them and watches their actions, much to his pleasure. It is while he is watching them that an elder approaches him, sees what he's watching and then predicts that he will one day find the most handsome man in the land. Of course, for convenience, the land extends beyond the borders of Greece – it's amazing what license directors take. And so starts Jason voyage of discovery.

"I'm so happy that you got the part and that you're working again," said Mitchell, when he met up with Chad the day before shooting started.

"You don't know how happy I am," I reiterated. "And with your blessing, I'm happy to be working with Chris, he seems a really great guy and you're very lucky to have him as a partner."

It was just coincidence that the day before we started to shoot, my dad popped around to see me, in fact is seemed as though everyone knew of my pending success because Hank also popped around. Fortunately he and my dad never arrived at the same time. My dad was the first to arrive, on his way home from work. He dropped in for a quick drink and to see how I was doing. Naturally the boys were already busy trading down below when he arrived, but that didn't seem to worry him. I think he was becoming used to the area in which I lived.

"I'm starting a new film tomorrow Dad. It's with a different company and I'm really looking forward to it."

"What's this one called, son; if it's got a title?"

"It's based on Greek mythology, Dad. It's the story of Jason and the Argonauts. Did you ever read it?"

"No, son, it wasn't part of my education so I have no idea what it's about."

I thought this very fortunate then I could bullshit my dad about the story line.

"What's it about, son?"

"It's about this Greek guy who goes on a quest around the world and he fights off terrible monsters."

"Sounds like fun," replied my dad. "What's he searching for?"

"We haven't got that far yet, Dad. It's still the early days and you know how film directors work; back to front."

I hoped that he would be satisfied with my answer and not delve any deeper. He wander over to the lounge window with his drink and peered down into the street.

"The boys seem to be busy tonight."

I walked over to where he was standing and also looked down. He was right, cars were running up and down the street and boys were negotiating constantly. It interested me to think that my dad took so much notice of the boys in the street, but I didn't know why. I had realized that every time he had come to my apartment, he had spent some time watching them, yet he never really spoke about their activities.

"I feel for some of those boys," I said, without thinking.

"Hm," said my dad, as though in deep thought. "I do too, son. It's a hard life being on the street like that and not knowing where your next dollar's coming from."

I was stunned by my father's statement. I would have thought most adults would have condemned the boys on the street, but not my father. He seemed to show a sense of compassion and I began to realize how much like him I was. I also knew that I was getting closer to telling him of my situation, but I wasn't sure if it was just a phase I was going through.

After he'd finished his drink, he hugged me and said his goodbyes and left. I watched as he walked to his car and saw some of the boys approach him and probably proposition him. While I watched him being propositioned, a strange thing happened. I saw Hank approach my dad. They stood and talked for some time and then I saw my dad put his hand into his pocket and hand something to Hank, but I couldn't make out what it was, then he headed off to his car, climbed in and set off home.

Half an hour later, there was a knock on my front door. I knew it was Hank because for some reason, known only to him, he never rang the door bell, but knocked instead. I opened the door to a smiling Hank, whom I invited in.

"Hi Hank, how's business?"

"Fine, fine Chad. I've already made $50 tonight without having to do anything."

"That's good, but how?"

"This dude I saw was walking to his car I think, so I approached him and asked him if he wanted me to give him a blow-job, 'cause you know how good I am at that, so he says no thanks but he puts his hand into his pocket and pulls out a $50 bill and gives it to me. How's that for kindness – or stupidity."

I smiled a thoughtful smile and said, "That was really good of the guy to do that."

"Hey listen" said Hank, changing the subject, "Joe was asking about you the other day. I think you made an impact on the dude. Where have you been?"

"Hank I've got myself another part in a movie, so I'll be off the streets for a while."

"Hey I like that, but even the guys down there," he said, pointing down towards the street, "they were asking for you. I think they like you. They think you're cool."

"Thanks Hank, I appreciate the flattery, but at the moment, I'm going to be OK financially."

He looked a little despondent.

"So you only come to us when you want money, is that it?"

"No, it's not like that, Hank."

"Well, it looks like it to me."

"I promise it's not. There might be nights when I'm not shooting scenes when I can come down and look for a bit of trade with you."

His face lit up again and he looked very seriously at me before saying, "You'll only go with me and none of the other guys?"

"You mean if a trick picks you up, then we go together?"

"Yeah. I like it like that."

I smiled at his simplicity.

"It's a deal, Hank," I said, shaking his hand as a sign of agreement.

"Chad, do you think I could stay the night here?"

I smiled at his request as I knew that he liked my company and I was flattered by it, but I was also aware that this could become a habit.

"Sure Hank, but no funny business."

"You know I wouldn't do anything like that."

"Hank! Don't bullshit me. I know that the minute to get into my bed, your hands begin to wander all over the place."

"I can't help it if I like what you've got."

"Your problem is you're in love with my cock and nothing else."

Hank blushed as he knew I was right.

"Do you blame me?" was his only retort. "I promise I won't touch you, but it'll probably kill me and you wouldn't like that, would you?"

I liked his innocent sense of humor and really, he was a sweet kid, although there wasn't much difference in our ages, he just seemed more immature than I was.

"Right, buddy, I'm off to bed early because I've got filming in the morning."

CHAPTER 13

JASON AND HIS ARGONAUTS

The day arrived, Hank was sent on his way and the cab was soon whizzing me off to the studio. When I arrived, I was glad to see Chris as I didn't know any of the others. However, soon Brad arrived and introduced everyone. We were going to shoot two scenes on the first day, and these included the market scene with two young guys, named Phil and Troy and then we were to shoot my sword fight scene.

"People, I'd like to welcome you all to the first day of shooting of *Jason and the Argonauts*," said Brad, addressing everyone. "The entire duration of our filming shouldn't last longer than a week or two, depending on how well you act and how few times we have to re-shoot scenes. After shooting is completed we'll be busy with the editing and unless anything untoward goes wrong, we won't have to call any of you back."

Brad gave a few more instructions and then it was time for those in the opening scenes to get into costume. I made my way to the costume room, found my 'skirt' and Speedo-like briefs and got dressed.

In the opening scene, I was to watch Troy and Phil make out in a workshop. The set designers had made a good job of creating a market place with a workshop in it. Within the workshop area, was a pile of hay in which the two young boys were to romp and there was a slightly secluded spot in which I was to hide and watch them.

"Chad, while you are watching them, although you have no dialogue, you need to act all the time because although the camera is focused on them, you'll also be in shot, so no rubbing your face or jerking off or anything like that. I only want to see your reactions to their antics," said Brad from his director's chair.

Troy and Phil appeared on the set and I looked at them in their costumes. Both looked so young but Chris had assured me that nobody on the set was under the age of eighteen. I found Troy more attractive than Phil and thought Phil had very little going for him, but I was soon to be proved wrong. The two stripped each other and began rolling in the haystack, and it was then that I saw Phil's reason for being in the movie. The boy had a long, thin uncut cock that hung well below his balls and I was surprised that such a skinny guy had such a long cock. As I watched them screwing, I was amazed at how aroused I became, and although it became difficult for me not to stroke myself, I didn't need any acting; my expressions were natural and fitting to what was going on between the two young boys.

After they had completed their scene, to Brad's approval, it was time for my sword fight scene. A handsome young man, by the name of Marc, appeared. He was dressed like a soldier, but he was representing a Roman soldier, which, when I asked Chris, was no differently dressed from the Mesopotamian soldiers.

Marc was a good-looking, trim and obviously well-hung young man. I say well-hung because under his Roman leather skirt I could see his Speedo-like briefs were bulging. He also wore a leather harness across his chest which was broad and well-defined. We were to have a sword fight and Brad had arranged for us to use real swords, so it meant we had to rehearse the fight scene so as not to kill each other. I can't place my finger on it, but there was something about Marc that attracted him to me. He seemed a gentle sort of person, yet physically he could have played the role of Jason. Once we had rehearsed to Brad's satisfaction, we got down to the actual filming.

"Chad, you and Marc are to fight and then you have to get him to the ground. When he's on the ground, you're going to 'ravage' him," said Brad in earnest.

I looked at Marc and in my mind; I liked the idea of ravaging him.

"Action!" shouted Brad, and Marc and I began our sword fight.

We began off very carefully not wanting to hurt each other, but at one point our swords got locked and we were up close to each other. We were face to face and I could feel Marc's warm breath on my face, but at the same time I could feel his hard-on press up against me. Suddenly I lost concentration and my sword slipped, cutting him on the bicep. Marc immediately fell to the ground and clutched his bicep.

"Cut!" shouted Brad, who rushed forward to see that Marc was not badly injured.

I felt terrible about hurting him, but we could see that it wasn't something serious and soon the medic had him cleaned up and had stopped the bleeding.

"Right, let's carry on with this scene," said Brad, returning to his director's chair, "but I think let's start it where you're already on the ground, Marc. Chad I want you to lean over him with your sword ready to pierce him, look into his face, drop your sword on the ground and then go into the action."

I knelt on the ground next to Marc and again apologized to him.

"Hey it's nothing. It was probably my fault," he said.

I smiled back and added, "Yes it was your fault. It was that big package you're carrying there."

Marc grinned and I was glad to see he was forgetting about his pain.

"Action!" shouted Brad.

I did as I had been instructed and dropped my sword but before I could do anything, I felt Marc grab hold of my crotch. I can't deny that I had already thrown a boner and my cock was straining to break free. Marc squeezed my shaft and I groaned with pleasure. Immediately I grabbed hold of his leather harness and hoisted him up so that we were once again face to face. I moved straight to his lips and clamped my mouth on his, my tongue searching in his open mouth until our tongues connected. I then slipped my hand between his thighs and felt the thick, long shaft waiting for attention. I ripped off his Speedo briefs and dropped down onto his circumcised cock. I took it all the way down my throat and sucked. Marc's body quivered as I sucked and his moans were loud and passionate as his body writhed from my touches. Soon we were both naked and my cock was ravaging his tight little ass. Our arms, mouths and hands were everywhere. I had never experienced passion like I did with Marc and in fact, I'd never experienced a connection with any guy on a first 'date'; not that this was a date.

We both sensed each other's heightened passion and when we were ready to explode, there was no warning to the other person; we fired our load together. My cock expanded and fired into his warm chute while he sent spasms of cum high into the air and onto his stomach, chest and me. As we slowly came down to earth, our kisses were gentle yet still deep and passionate until we lay in each other's arms, our breathing slowly returning to normality.

A feeble "cut" came from Brad and then there was wild applause from those around watching. Marc and I lay still, looking into each other's eyes and smiling contently. I was still embedded in him and felt my cock continually throbbing as he extracted every last drop of my seed with his tight ass muscles.

"You're one helluva fuck," I whispered into Marc's ear.

"So are you. Next time your ass is mine."

I grinned at him and winked. We had connected.

A crew member ran up to us with a couple of towels which we wrapped around ourselves and went off to shower and clean ourselves.

"That's a wrap," we heard Brad say as we left. "I'm even considering changing this scene to the end of the movie and making Marc the man that Jason eventually finds and settles down with. I've never seen a scene like that where there was so much passion and no acting."

When we reached the showers, Marc already had his hands on me and I was ready for round two. We stood under the shower of water and let it splash over our bodies while our mouths searched each other's body and our hard cocks played together. Although no sex occurred in the shower, we arranged to go back to my apartment and have dinner together, and whatever else might come with the dinner.

CHAPTER 14

SOMETHING NOT PLANNED

The following day at the studio, people were watching to see how Marc and I interacted because some knew that he was coming back to my place for dinner.

"How was last night?" asked an inquisitive Chris, who I'm sure was dying to hear the latest scandal.

"Dinner was very pleasant, thanks, and so was the company."

"Did Marc stay the night?"

I grinned at Chris.

"You'd really love to know, wouldn't you? Yes, actually he did and we fucked all night until the sun came up this morning; first I fucked him and then he fucked me and that's how it went on all night."

I could see the shock on Chris's face; unsure whether to believe me or not.

"Are you serious, Chad?"

"Absolutely. We took turns in fucking each other; after all it's only fair that we do that, don't you think?"

"But I thought you were a top and never bottomed for anyone."

"Hey, there's nothing like a change occasionally," I casually answered, without hinting whether I was telling the truth or not.

I told Marc what I'd said so he agreed to play along, and very soon it was all around the studio that Marc and I had taken turns in fucking the other. Faces were lighting up in the thought that they too might get lucky with one of us, but we ignored all the gossip.

The schedule for the day was to film Jason's journey to Egypt in search of his ideal man and for this the set constructers had built a barge and painted a backdrop depicting the river Nile with a couple of pyramids in the background. It looked very effective, but as most of the action was to take place inside of the barge, they served little purpose other than to set the scene for the viewer.

I was back in my crazy Grecian skirt with its Speedo brief underneath, but today's actors playing opposite me was to be a young African-American boy who was playing a slave. I was to be joined by someone who represented a wealthy Egyptian nobleman on whose barge we were traveling. A series of boys were dressed up to represent slaves rowing the barge, while Joshua, the African-American stood by with a long pole on which was attached a spray of ostrich feathers acting as a fan. Joshua had on a white skirt, similar to mine, but was topless. They sprayed his chest, arms and back with a thin layer of oil so that he shone like bronze in the light, and the guy playing the nobleman, had on a long white toga, very much like the Romans wore, so I wasn't sure whether the costume department had got their clothing mixed up or there was a shortage of Egyptian dress.

We were called by Brad to take up our positions and the slaves lined the side of the barge while the nobleman, played by a boy called Sam, Joshua and I, took up our positions under a canopy that represented a secluded spot. Sam and I lay on thick, puffy cushions while Joshua stood behind us, gently waving the pole with the ostrich feathers.

Some very basic and mundane dialogue had been written for us and we'd learnt it, but in actual fact it could have been possible to have said anything, because it didn't matter.

Brad called, "Action", and the cameras started rolling.

Sam and I chattered about the weather and our journey to the source of the Nile in search of a perfect young man and the slaves pretended they were rowing the barge along its journey. Joshua, in the meanwhile stood waving his fan, legs firmly planted apart and where I lay, I had the perfect view up his short skirt to the bulge hidden under it. Sam pretended to be drinking wine from a chalice and eventually became drunk and passed out, leaving me to Joshua, and the other slaves, should the urge take me.

Once Sam had 'passed out', I lay back to enjoy the view, not of the Nile, but of Joshua and what he had to offer. The idea was for me to watch him and begin to stroke my crotch teasingly, to get his attention. Then I was to summon him to place himself between my legs and to please me.

"Slave! Come hither," I commanded.

I told you the dialogue was terrible because I'm sure neither Grecians nor Egyptians said 'hither'.

"Come hither slave and lay your head between my mighty thighs where you will see the empires of the western world and you can taste the fruits of my journeys."

What a load of crap, I thought, but we had to say these stupid lines.

Joshua put down his fan and did as he was commanded. He had a shaved head so when he rested his head on my lap, I was able to rub my hand over his smooth scalp. Joshua positioned himself so that his head was on my crotch for easy access to his mouth and if I needed to, I could lift my legs and wrap them around his upper back.

Once he was in position, he spoke his lines.

"My lord, your thighs are like the great timbers on Mount Lebanon."

I smiled to show my approval while his head rested on my crotch. I could feel how the pressure of his head was pushing onto my cock and arousing it.

"My lord, I think I see some of the fruit of your journeys."

I felt his tongue run across the Lycra briefs I was wearing. His tongue had a rough texture to it and it grazed across my shaft, bringing me to a greater arousal.

"My lord, would you like me to taste some of the fruit you have to offer?"

"I would like that slave."

Joshua slowly lowered the waistband of my briefs and allowed my cut cock to peer over the top. His tongue licked the tip of my cock causing it to throb and he cleaned away the shiny pre-cum that had accumulated there.

"My lord you have a sweet taste which pleases me." What you do pleases me slave. What is your name, slave?"

"Anouk, my lord."

"That is a name befitting a strong man like you. You have the body of one who is strong and what else do you possess, Anouk?"

"As you have strong wood here my lord," said Joshua, pointing to my crotch, "so do I my lord."

"Anouk, it would please me to see your wood if you will allow."

"To please you my lord, I shall reveal it."

He slid off his briefs and produced a beautiful brown cock, long and thick with a smooth head and a veiny shaft.

"You have a truly wonderful piece there Anouk. I am sure many men envy that which you possess and therefore I would like to touch and taste your fruits."

Joshua positioned himself closer to me so that my mouth could gain access to his cock and as I opened my mouth, so he sank his cock into the depths of my throat. I loved his taste and salivated over it.

"You taste of the Nile and its magic, Anouk. Your wood is fine and sturdy and I feel that it has a place in me"

As I said this, I realized it was not what was in the script. I had changed the wording somehow and everyone in the know, knew that I'd said the wrong thing, but let the scene continue. I noticed a slight look of surprise from Joshua, but he played along.

"Does my lord desire me to place my wood with him?"

"He would like that, Anouk."

"If it pleases my lord, would you lie on your side so that my wood may be prepared for you?"

I rolled onto my side and waited for Joshua to sink his thick cock into my tight chute and let me have a taste of him.

Brad had said nothing neither had he stopped the cameras, so he must have been happy with the plan.

I felt the tip of Joshua's cock nudge my asshole and I spread my ass cheeks to allow him entry, then I felt the slow push as he tried to insert his hard cock into my waiting opening. I pushed back to meet his thrust and felt the bulbous head break through and enter my tunnel.

"Aargh! That feels good Anouk. I like the feel of your wood. It is so smooth that it flows in me like the River Nile flows."

Joshua started a slow, rhythmic thrust and pull motion and each time he sank into me I pushed back and enjoyed the deep penetration that was taking place.

Throughout our action, the other slaves were supposed to be 'rowing' but in actual fact every eye was on us as Joshua made Egyptian love to me.

Finally, when both of us had come and were relaxing from our experience together, Brad shouted "Cut!"

"That wasn't what I expected, but I must say I enjoyed it so we'll keep it in – the scene, that is, not Joshua's cock!"

I thanked Joshua and we both got up and went off to clean ourselves, leaving the others to debate the incident that they had just witnessed. As we stood under the showers, I admired his glistening body and relished in the thought that I was meeting some really hunky guys on this set and who knew, we might remain friends for ever.

The days that followed were filled with sex, which is understandable as this was a sex movie we were making, but I made some interesting observations.

I'm not usually in the habit of comparing sexual partners, but I must say that when I did my scene with Chris, I was somewhat disappointed. Maybe it was because I had got to know him and Mitchell and doing a scene with Mitchell was very enjoyable, but when it came to Chris, I realized that he was one of those young boys who, if you saw him in a crowd, would disappear into that crowd.

He had been cast as a Mesopotamian soldier, well they were obviously not in the same league as the Roman soldiers because Chris looked insignificant and 'skinny' compared to Marc as the Roman soldier. The scene involved me having to take Chris captive and then punish him by tying him up and fucking him. That all sounds very exciting, but when it came to doing the scene, I found Chris weak, not very responsive and I didn't think he worked his ass very well. Now I know he'll probably read this, so I'm sorry for saying these things, but they were true. I was unimpressed with him in bed. Maybe when he's off screen, he might be different or when he's with Mitchell, but on screen it was probably the most uninspiring scene I had shot.

I had thought it quite a turn-on tying Chris up and watching him squirm, but he didn't; it almost felt as if he did this on a regular basis and he was now bored of doing it. I noticed he even battled to get a hard-on, which most guys don't have a problem with, especially if someone's plowing your ass with a solid, hard cock, but poor Chris battled. We had to re-shoot a number of his scenes because he couldn't get it up. Maybe he was nervous, but then this was not his first film. However, having said that, I still think Chris is a very sweet young man and it's obvious that he and Mitchell make a good couple.

Brad was correct about his idea as to how long shooting would take. Within two weeks we had completed all the scenes and now it was up to the editing department to put the movie together. Before the actors all departed, he told us to stay in touch as there might have to be re-shoots if problems arose and that he was going to have a private screening in three weeks' time if all went well.

Leaving everyone was quite traumatic in the sense that some of us had become very close and were bonding like a family. Others knew that they were contracted to do another movie straight away so they never worried about the departure of people, but I was not in that category.

"Will I see you again?" I asked Marc, as we prepared to leave the studio for possibly the last time.

"I sure as hell hope so," he said, with determination in his voice. "I want to get into that cute ass of yours again and again."

I smiled at the thought and I knew that if he was that determined, then I'd also get another chance to get a taste of his tight ass.

When I left in the cab, I saw Joshua standing at the entrance to the studio.

"Do you want a lift, Josh?"

"Where you going?" he asked.

"Back to my place. We can share a cab if you like or you can come back to my place."

He thought for a moment and then said, "Can I come back to your place?"

"Sure," I replied nonchalantly, but with a sense of excitement running through my mind.

He climbed in alongside me in the back of the cab and we headed back to my place, to do you know what!!

CHAPTER 15

A RIGHT ROYAL TEA PARTY

After we had finished the filming and after Josh had left my place having enjoyed the tastes of my body and I his, I phoned my dad to see how he was as I hadn't seen him for a while, me being busy filming.

"Chad, your mother's been nagging me to bring her round to your place; I think she's missing you. Do you think I can bring her and Gran around some time?"

"Sure Dad, what about after you finish work, you can pop around with them for tea or a snack in the early evening because I know Gran doesn't like being out late."

"How about tonight because I finish work early today so we could be at your place by 4:30, if that's OK with you?"

"That's fine by me, Dad, but just warn Mum of the area; you know what she's like when she doesn't see up-market shops and instead sees a little bit of rough hanging around."

My dad burst out laughing at my description.

"I know exactly what you mean, son, don't worry, I'll sort her out."

I replaced the telephone receiver and started to panic. Neither my mum nor my grandmother had seen my apartment, let alone the area, so it was natural that an element of panic set in. I started to tidy up and hoped that Hank wouldn't pay an unexpected visit while they were here. While I was busy, the phone rang again. I thought it might be my dad having forgotten to tell me something, but instead it was Mitchell.

"Hi buddy, how's the star?"

"Ha, ha! Who are you talking about? I'm no star just a currently out of work actor now."

"I believe you were very good in the movie and you set quite a few hearts fluttering, so Chris says."

I wondered how much of that was the truth. The only heart that I know was fluttering was Marc's because we did tend to hit it off together.

"Don't talk shit. There weren't any hearts fluttering like you say."

"Don't you believe it! You're a star among some of those actors – you and that big dick of yours."

"Sounds like you're just trying to be nice so you can get that big dick again."

"I wouldn't mind and I think you know that, but enough of this crap, the reason I phoned was because we wanted to know if you'd like to pop round tonight for dinner with us?"

"Mitchell, I'd love to but my Dad's just phoned and he's bringing my mum and Gran around tonight. Could I possibly take a rain check on your date."

"Not a problem," said Mitchell, sounding a little despondent. "I'll tell you what, if they leave early, why not come round for a drink, then?"

"That sounds OK to me. Usually my Gran doesn't like being out late, so they might go fairly early, but I'll give you a call either way and let you know."

"Then maybe we'll see you later. Cheers for now, buddy."

As I replaced the receiver, I thought of what Mitchell had said and wondered if he really meant what he'd said. Maybe my popularity was growing and maybe there were some guys who fancied me.

At 5:00p.m, the family arrived. Dad's expression told me so much without him having to open his mouth.

"Hi Mum. Hi Gran, welcome to my little home," I said spreading my arms to embrace them.

Mum gave me a peck on the check and sailed past on her search of discovery, while Gran stood mystified by the place.

"I'm not happy with this area," said my Mum, surveying the lounge and my furnishings. "There are a lot of funny people around here," she continued, looking for dust and rearranging objects of display.

"Jane, leave the boy's things alone. He's put things there because he likes them there. This is his home, not ours," said my dad, trying to put a stop to her mad rearranging campaign.

"Do you live here alone, my boy?" asked my Gran in a sotto voce voice; obviously the shock of the neighborhood was too much for her.

"Yes, Gran."

"It doesn't look very safe for you to be on your own," she rambled on. "Maybe you should get a friend to stay with you."

I wasn't sure just what Gran meant by that; whether she was concerned for my safety or whether dear Gran knew something about my sex life.

"I'm sure he's got plenty of friends who call round, haven't you Chad?" said my dad.

"Of course," I replied.

Except my dad had never seen any people here.

The search of discovery continued with my mum leading the way and poor Gran stumbling along behind and my dad and I bringing up the rear. Into the kitchen we went, cupboards being opened to inspect the quantity and type of food in store, then the fridge was examined and from there we headed into the bathroom where the bath was inspected to see if it had a dirt ring in it. I knew my mother was looking for any excuse to take me back home again.

"Who cleans your apartment, Chad?" asked my mother getting into the shower cubicle to inspect.

"I do, Mum, and not a bad job, hey?"

No comment.

The toilet was flushed, not because it needed to be, but I think she wanted to see if it worked. She saw my wash basket and took the lid off to check what was inside.

"And the washing! Who does that?"

"I do sometimes; otherwise I take it to a laundry nearby."

She scratched through the dirty washing, pulling out a pair of my briefs and a shirt and then throwing them back into the basket.

Now we headed to my sanctum – the holy of holies – my bedroom. Thank goodness I had made up the bed and everything was in its right place. Mum and Gran stood in the center of the room and twirled. They seemed to be glued to one spot and turned around surveying the neatness and tidiness of the room. If they could only see it after I've had a rough session with some hunky man, they'd die.

Not to be outdone, my mother headed to my bedside table and pulled open the top drawer. She looked in then she dug her hand into it. Out came a handful of condoms and a tube of lube.

"And this!" she asked in horror.

I don't know who got more of a shock, her or me.

"A guy can't be too careful these days, Mum. You have to take precautions you know," I answered.

Dad's face was a picture of delight. I could see he wanted to burst out laughing but knew better. If he had, my mother would have torn into him verbally. The condoms and lube were dramatically thrown back into the drawer and it was slammed shut. I could see my mother was not a happy lady so I decided to say something.

"Mum, if you didn't always make it your mission to go peering into other people's things, you wouldn't be so shocked and you wouldn't have to concern yourself with their lives."

She gave me an indignant look and strutted out and went to the lounge. Gran tapped me on the arm.

"Son, I think you've got yourself a very nice apartment, but I do worry about you. I really think you need to get a friend. When we arrived I saw quite a number of young boys downstairs, do they live in this building as well?"

I looked at my dad but he never budged. I wondered if he was going to say something about the boys or not.

"No, Gran."

"Well, maybe one of them might like to stay with you here."

I couldn't believe what my grandmother was saying. If only she knew what those young boys were doing down in the street, she might have second thoughts. In the meantime, my mother had made herself comfortable on the couch in the lounge.

"Are we getting something to drink or must I get it myself?"

My mother was the sort of person who liked to get her own way and was constantly trying to control what everyone else did. This I had established as I got older and I often wondered how my dad put up with it.

"What would you like, Mum?" I asked politely.

"Tea, please," came the indignant reply.

"And you Gran?"

"Nothing as mundane as tea, Chad, darling. I think something stronger if you don't mind."

I smiled when I heard my Gran ask for something stronger. Maybe she felt she needed it with my Mum around.

"Whiskey, beer, martini, gin … water!"

"Certainly not water," she replied with a steely look.

I liked my Gran even though there were times when I thought she emulated my mother.

"What about you, Dad?"

"Do you have a beer, Chad?"

"Absolutely, I'll get them for you."

I headed into the kitchen and soon found my dad behind me.

"Can't you take the pace in the lounge, hey?"

"When your mother gets going, there's no stopping her, so I thought I'd leave her and your Gran together."

I busied myself making my Gran a martini while the kettle boiled for my mother's tea.

"I was thinking about what your Gran said; maybe it might be a good idea to take in one of those boys as a tenant. It would halve the rent for you."

"But Dad…"

"I know it would be a little risky as they don't earn money regularly, but at least you would have company."

Now I was completely bewildered by my Dad's ideas.

"But Dad …"

"I know they're hustlers, son, but they're also young boys who have very little future."

"I don't have much future either, Dad. My job's risky too you know."

"That's why you need someone to stay with you and help pay the rent, if you'll excuse the pun."

The kettle began to whistle so I started to pour the water in the tea cup.

"A few days back, I saw you talk to one of the boys down there when you left my apartment."

"Yes," laughed my Dad, "he'd propositioned me; me at my age being propositioned."

"And what's wrong with that, you're still good looking for your age," I replied.

"Yes, he offered me a blow job. Can you believe it?"

Oh yes, I could believe anything that Hank did.

"So why didn't you agree to his offer," I jokingly asked.

My dad looked seriously at me, then with a straight face, answered, "I had nowhere to go and neither did he."

I immediately burst out laughing, but at first I thought my dad was serious as he never had a grin on his face, then he joined in with my laughter. The two of us laughed and laughed until a shrill voice cut through of fun.

"What's happening in the kitchen? Where's my tea?"

Dad and I looked at each other and sniggered softly. I thought this might be the right time to test my dad.

"What would you say if it was me down there on that street, Dad, hustling to make ends meet?"

His eyes softened when he looked at me before answering.

"I'd still love you, son."

I didn't know how to respond, but it did give me an insight into my dad's feelings. He'd never actually used the words 'love you' before, but I did appreciate his saying them now.

"I know you're very independent and if you were short of money and you chose to hustle to make a living, it wouldn't worry me. What would worry me would be your safety. I wouldn't want any harm to come to you."

I was shocked to hear this and it made me wonder if he already knew something of my escapades, but I wasn't about to expand on our conversation. The tea was poured, Gran's martini was ready and I'd got a beer for Dad and me; then we headed back into the lounge.

"We like your apartment, Chad," said my Gran sipping her martini and licking her lips. "Ooh! I haven't had one of these for quite some time."

"When you say 'we' Gran does that mean you and Mum?" I enquired.

Before she could reply, my mother interjected.

"I like your apartment; it's just the neighborhood that worries me."

"Mum, you don't have to worry. I've got to know almost everyone around here, even some of the boys down in the street."

"Well there you go," said Gran with gusto, draining her martini glass and waving it about to suggest a refill. "I told you to ask one of those young boys to share the apartment with you.

A stony stare greeted my Gran as my mother glared at her.

"Now tell us about your job; that is if you have one," said my mother.

I hesitated as I thought just how I was going to elaborate to them on my filming career.

"I'm busy shooting a movie called *Jason and the Argonauts*," I said, very proudly. "It set in Greece in the ancient times," I continued.

My mother gave me one of her tired looks.

"And what are you, dear?" queried my Gran.

"I'm Jason, Gran."

"Ooh! That's wonderful. So you are the star, then?"

"No, the star Gran. I just play the main character."

"So that means you're the star," she insisted. "And when do we see it?"

'Never' I wanted to say. Can you imagine what my mother and grandmother would think seeing me in the nude and especially the scenes where I'm romping with other naked men.

"You know, Chad, it worries me that you seem very secretive about the things you do," said my mother, taking another sip of her tea.

"It's just that I didn't think you'd be interested, Mum."

At last my Dad came to my rescue.

"Leave the boy alone, Jane, he doesn't have to tell us everything, after all, he's an adult now."

"I like to know what my son is up to?" replied my mother, almost in a tone reprimanding my dad.

"I just like to get on with my own life, Mum. I don't come asking you where you've been or what you're doing, do I? I respect your privacy."

"You see how the youth of today are turning out?" retorted my mother, to whoever wanted to listen to her.

My Mum gulped down her tea and stood up.

"I think we ought to be going. It's getting late and I don't want to be found hanging around in this area late at night."

Both my Dad and Gran looked bewildered by my Mum's remark but they new that they had no say in the matter. Both my Dad and Gran gulped down their drinks and followed my mother's instructions. They rose, hugged and kissed me and departed, leaving my Dad to say his goodbyes.

"Goodbye son. Take care of yourself and some of the boys down there," he said, giving me a kiss on the cheek and hugging me to him.

It was amazing to feel my Dad embrace me, like he'd done when I was a small child, but now we were both adults. I held him tightly to me, letting our embrace linger. I felt that there was something that my Dad was hiding from me but didn't want to discuss, yet I thought that he wanted to say something.

Without thinking, I said, "Any time you want to talk, Dad, just pop by."

I wanted to laugh because to me that was the sort of comment that a father might say to his child, and not the other way around.

We released our grasp on each other, smiled and he left.

CHAPTER 16

THE PREMIERE

I was very pleased that Brad had not phoned me back to re-shoot any scenes, but having said that, I was also sad about it, because had he called us back, I might have been able to enjoy the company of Marc. The only contact that Brad had made was to tell me that the editing was completed and that the movie was print-ready. He had organized to have a premiere in three days time and the whole cast, as well as some other people connected in the film industry were also invited. I wondered if Mr. Hamilton might just be one of those 'other' people. I had phoned Chris to find out if he and Mitchell had been invited, which they had, and to find out from Chris, what we were expected to do. After all, I'd never been to a film premiere, let alone be the star in a film.

The evening of the premiere, which was to take place at 7:00p.m, arrived. I had showered, dressed and called a cab to fetch me and when I arrived at the studio, there were quite a few of the cast already waiting.

Drinks and light snacks had been provided in one of the rehearsal rooms, which had been decorated a la Grecian and prior to the viewing, we had been invited to partake in snacks and drinks while Brad was to give a short presentation on the making of the film.

Chris and Mitchell were already at the studio when I arrived. Naturally there was much hugging and kissing between the guests and I was interested to see if Joshua and Marc brought anyone with them.

"Didn't you bring a partner?" asked Mitchell, showing mock surprise.

"I thought of bringing my Dad," I replied with a straight face.

Naturally, neither Chris nor Mitchell knew whether I was telling the truth or having them on, and so they didn't broach the subject.

Joshua was the first, of the two men I had fancied, to arrive. He came along with another dark-skinned young man who looked more Latino than African-American and who he introduced as Miguel.

Miguel was lean and tall with a striking smile and a flash of white teeth. When he spoke he had an accent that reminded me of a Jamaican, although Joshua had said he was from San Juan. The two men seemed pretty close, but then I could understand Miguel sticking to Joshua, because he didn't know anyone else at the premiere.

Joshua, Miguel and I stood drinking cocktails and munching on snacks, while Chris and Mitchell had wandered off to 'mingle' among the 'rich and famous', so they said.

I looked around but didn't notice either rich or famous, unless they hadn't arrived yet, but in the meantime, Miguel and I were getting along very well. When I had the chance, I got Joshua on his own and asked him what the setup was between him and Miguel.

"Do you like him, Chad?" enquired Joshua.

"I didn't want to say yes until I'd established their relationship; I mean I didn't want to put my foot in it and say 'yes' and then find out that they were deeply involved.

"So where does Miguel fit into your life, Josh?"

"He's just a very good friend," he replied.

That was good as it meant that if I wanted to make a move on Miguel, I could; I say IF!

"Tell me more, Josh."

"I've known him for about two years now and we're just good buddies."

"Good buddies or GOOD buddies?" I asked. "And when I say GOOD, I mean are you two into each other?"

Josh laughed at my fumbled way of trying to find out information.

"If you mean does Miguel sleep with me, the answer is yes and no. Does that answer your question?"

Naturally the 'yes' and 'no' confused me. Maybe they did sleep together on occasions and maybe they were closer than Josh was making out to me and they spent more time in each other's bed.

Miguel pricked up his ears when he heard his name mentioned.

"Are you two talking about me?"

"No!" I rapidly answered.

"Yes!" cut in Josh.

"Well is it yes or no?" asked Miguel with a sparkle in his eye

"Yes we were talking about you. I was asking Josh about you."

"And…?" Enquired Miguel.

I was stumped. I didn't know how to respond. I couldn't tell them I fancied Miguel and I couldn't tell them that even better, I fancied both of them.

Just then Marc suddenly appeared.

Oh shit! I couldn't tell anyone I also fancied Marc. Hell, I was a slut!

"Hi guys," said the jovial Marc as he reached us. "How are things?"

"Fine, fine!" I replied, giving him a hug.

Josh also hugged Marc and then introduced him to Miguel. Immediately I saw a spark between them but I wasn't sure whether it was just a friendly spark or a FRIENDLY spark! And then there were four.

We stood chatting together, without any others joining us until Brad arrived to make his little speech.

"Ladies and Gentlemen," said Brad to the assembled crowd.

At first I thought he was being facetious by saying 'Ladies' as I hadn't seen any and I thought he might be referring to some of us; then I saw three ladies huddled together.

"I would like to welcome you all to *Virilis Films* and thank you for sharing this event with us. Before we get down to the business of watching the movie, there are a few people I would like to introduce to you. The first of these is my right-hand man and chief editor Matt Curling."

Matt stepped forward and received sporadic applause.

"Then I would like you to meet our faithful backer, who, without his money, none of this would have taken place; Mr. Jermyn Le Mutt."

A heftily built African-American stepped forward and he too received applause, but a little more than Matt received.

"And now, Ladies and Gentlemen, I would like you to meet the star of our film *Jason and the Argonauts,* Jason himself, Chad Patterson."

I didn't expect to be singled out, but as I walked towards Brad, I felt very proud of my achievement. I was greeted with a warm applause and a few whistles, obviously from the Argonauts who had found me a friendly, sexy guy to work with. Now if that isn't confidence, I don't know what is!

After the introductions, Brad invited all the guests to go into his private viewing cinema to watch the movie for the first time.

I sat with Josh, Miguel and Marc, the four of us like excited kids. The lights went down and the film flickered onto the screen. The music started and Jason began his journey to find the perfect man.

Throughout the running of the film, there were a few comments from members of the audience; snide comments and praiseworthy ones. \there were even gasps when I first appeared naked and then there were whistles when the sex scenes became hot and steamy. I must admit, but not publicly, that there were quite a few moments when, as I watched, I found myself becoming aroused by the scene. At one stage, during the scene with Josh, he laid his hand on my knee and looked at me. I felt a gentle squeeze and returned the look.

The director and editor had cut and spliced scenes so that the ending involved Marc and me in our famous sword fighting scene because they felt that the passion shown between the two of us was so intense that this was obviously the guy that Jason thought was the perfect man for him – and they lived happily ever after!

As the credits came up, there was spontaneous applause and a great deal of back-slapping. Everyone seemed pleased with the result, me included. I was impressed by the way I had come across on the screen and wondered if anyone in my family would ever see this film and would appreciate the role I'd played. I didn't have time to wonder for long, as Josh suggested that the four of us go for drinks after the viewing. As there was nothing else planned, we left the studio and headed for a local bar to celebrate our success.

The bar that we had selected was crowded and some of Josh's friends were there, so when they saw him together with Miguel and Marc and me, they flocked around us to see who the new guys were. They seemed such a friendly group of guys and soon we were all chatting, drinking and laughing, without a care in the world.

"What are you going to do now, Chad?" asked Marc, as he stood next to me at the bar counter, sipping our beers.

I hadn't thought about the future. I was too busy taking in the present. I suddenly went silent as I faced the reality.

"I don't know," I replied, looking at him seriously.

"Do you have another contract with Brad?"

"No, so I suppose that puts me out of work. What about you?"

"I've got a two film contract so whatever he makes next, I'll be in it," replied Marc.

The sudden realization that I was back on the street, so to speak, hit home. Immediately I thought of the boys on the street and wondered if I would be joining Hank again.

"What are you looking so serious about?" asked Josh, noticing the anxiety in my face.

"Oh it's nothing," I replied casually. "I was just wondering what I would do now that I'm unemployed."

"You don't have to be," said a deep voice from my left hand side.

I turned to see who'd spoken and recognized the face. It was the guy who was the money behind our film, Jermyn Le Mutt.

"I'm sorry to interrupt you guys talking, but I overheard you saying that you were now unemployed and you didn't know what to do next. Am I right?"

I nodded.

"May we speak, Chad?"

"Sure, Mr. Le Mutt."

"Please call me Jermyn. Can I get you another drink?"

"Thanks, but I'm still busy."

"Well then would you guys mind if I borrowed Chad for a moment to talk privately with him?"

They all muttered that it wouldn't be a problem, and he led to a quiet corner of the bar where we could hear each other without having to raise our voices.

"Chad," said Jermyn, when we were out of earshot. "I liked you in the movie and I think you have all the goods, if you know what I mean…"

I smiled at the compliment.

"Well, I think I could offer you something, if you're willing to take up the offer."

He hesitated, allowing what he'd said to me to sink in.

"I think you'd be a very popular young man among my friends and others. I think you have class and above all, you have a very good body."

"Thank you, I appreciate the flattery."

"I'm not flattering you; I'm stating a fact. I would like you to work for me."

I looked surprised and added, "Doing what, Jermyn?"

"Pleasing men!"

I swallowed hard, because I thought I knew what he was getting at.

"You want me to hustle, is that what you're suggesting?"

"I want to manage you but you're not going to be one of these fly-by-night, low down the ladder hustlers; you're going to be classy and your clientele will be classy, not something off the street."

I remained quiet.

"What do you think?"

I knew I'd need money to survive and I knew that I could work alongside Hank, but this sounded like I could make better money.

"I honestly don't know what to say, Jermyn."

"I'll tell you what, come back to my place and let's discuss this in a more intimate atmosphere."

I knew he had money and I also knew he had contacts, but I didn't know what he was like as a boss. I thought for a moment and then smiled.

"Ok, let's go back to your place and take it from there."

I told the other guys that I was heading out and although Marc asked me where I was going, I merely said I'd contact him the following day and fill him in. With that, Jermyn and I left the bar.

CHAPTER 17

THE INTERVIEW

As we left the bar, with Jermyn's large hand on my shoulder, I wondered what I was heading to. His driver pulled up in a black car, which was one of those stretch limos, and the door was opened for us. Jermyn got in first and I followed. As we drove to his house, he chattered casually about the film, asking me how I had enjoyed making it.

"I loved every minute of it, Jermyn. It was fun and the people were great."

"You liked those boys?"

"Yes and I made some good friends there."

"Any that you fancy?"

I wasn't sure why he'd ask a question like that, so I replied that there was a couple without naming them.

"That's nice. They're a great bunch of guys."

Although it was dark, I noticed that when we drove through the gates to Jermyn's house, the grounds, which were well lit, looked immense. As to the house, it wasn't a house but more like a baronial mansion.

When we got inside of the mansion, Jermyn took me to his bedroom where he stripped off and ordered me to suck his long dick. There was no foreplay, just raw sex. I didn't have a problem with that as I enjoy dick, especially if it's long and cut, but it was when he ordered me to lie on my back and he rammed his hard cock deep into my ass that I became worried. His actions were frantic and rough. To him it seemed like an exercise that had to be got out of the way as soon as possible. This actually suited me as the pain was excruciating and I felt as though I was just being raped.

When he was finished, he got up and walked about me admiring my body and saying complimentary things about my abs and chest, cock and ass. I was more bewildered by his frantic actions than the compliments that were now flowing.

"I think you'll do well for me," he said, pulling on his boxer shorts and strutting out of the bedroom and downstairs to the lounge. "Come with me," he ordered. I followed down the stairs, wearing nothing but a contented look on my face.

The situation was weird. He sat in a huge wing-back chair in the lounge as though he was on a throne and I had to sit opposite him. He sat and stared at my flaccid cock as it lay casually on my left thigh.

"You've got yourself a good dick there, boy, but can you use it?"

Of course I could use it! I don't how many guys wanted my dick buried in their tight asses.

"Yes, I know how to use it, Jermyn."

He rang a bell and when the butler arrived he told him to get the driver to fetch Miguel.

I looked startled.

"Do you mean…?" I started to say.

"You liked him didn't you?"

"You mean Miguel from the premiere tonight?" I asked.

"The same. He's in my employ as well. I have sent for my driver to pick him up from the bar and bring him here. I want you to fuck him."

He was very direct and blunt. Of course I liked the idea of what Jermyn had planned, but there was no finesse or romance in the idea; it was pure unadulterated raw sex. I imagined that this was what Jermyn liked. When I thought of this, I wondered if he had ever had a relationship with anyone and if he had, how did he treat the person.

It didn't take the driver long to fetch Miguel and return him to the mansion. When he entered and saw me, there was a broad smile on his face. I could see he was happy to see me, just as I was happy to see him.

"Miguel, take yourself up to my room and get yourself ready," said Jermyn, without any explanation to the young man.

I therefore assumed that Miguel had done this sort of thing before and I wondered if I worked for Jermyn whether I would get the same treatment. Miguel did as he was requested, probably thinking that Jermyn was on his way up to the room, but instead, it was both of us making out way upstairs, five minutes after Miguel had left.

We walked into Jermyn's bedroom, which included a king size bed, and found Miguel lying face up with his legs spread open. His flaccid uncut cock lay casually across his left thigh. His slim stomach rose and sank gently as he breathed and his chest looked buffed. Jermyn walked over to the bed and slowly caressed Miguel's leg nearest to him. I noticed how Miguel's cock seemed to give a little movement as Jermyn's finger tips slid up the inner thigh towards the hefty balls.

"I have a special treat for you tonight," said Jermyn as his fingers reached Miguel's balls.

Miguel smiled charmingly at Jermyn.

"Chad is here for you tonight, but I'm staying to watch."

I was shocked when Jermyn said that he was going to watch, but I understood this to be like an interview, but one that is practical in nature. Miguel didn't seem to mind if Jermyn watched, so again I wondered if this was a common occurrence to Miguel. I was told to strip and to get onto the bed with Miguel, while Jermyn made himself comfortable in an easy chair he had in his bedroom. This was like watching a movie scene being enacted.

I stripped and as I was doing so, I admired Miguel's lithe body and at the same time I found myself getting aroused. By the time I had removed my briefs, I had a full erection and the sight of that excited Miguel. An instant quantity of blood flowed to his cock, making it stand upright and I noticed how his foreskin began to peel back, revealing his shiny cock head. I lowered myself onto the bed and my and Miguel's lips met as our bodies contorted against each other.

Throughout our love-making, I caught sight of Jermyn stroking his own cock as he watched us and as I lifted Miguel's legs to explore his fine ass, I noticed Jermyn stand up to get a closer look.

I decided that I liked Miguel so was not about to 'rape' him much like Jermyn had done to me. With Jermyn, there was no emotional, psychological or metaphysical action; it was just raw sex, but with Miguel, there were the emotions of care and kindness and I did think that he was very sweet, so I was gentle when I entered his warm body. I felt the tightness of his chute encompass my shaft and then tighten even more around my cock, bringing a sense of heightened pleasure to me.

Our passion didn't last long as we'd both brought each other to our climax quickly. When we had finished and had relaxed, our lips met once more and I thanked Miguel for the pleasure that he'd given me, and then I noticed the wet patch on the carpet to Jermyn's bedroom where he'd shot his load after we had both come.

I climbed from the bed and pulled on my briefs and clothes and waited for Jermyn to say something.

"What did you think, Miguel?" asked Jermyn.

Miguel smiled at me and nodded to Jermyn.

"Awesome," he replied.

"Thanks," was all Jermyn said, and then led me out, leaving Miguel in his bed.

"It seems you have passed the tests, Chad. I had felt your tight ass and I've seen you in action and I think there will definitely be a lot of people who will be craving your body."

Again I was flattered by the compliments but I was still unsure of my future with Jermyn; however, he seemed to have made up his mind that I was now his.

His driver was waiting for me at the entrance to the mansion and I was driven home. I noticed the driver kept eyeing me in the car's rear-view mirror. He looked a young guy and after seeing his looks, I ventured to ask him a question.

"What's it like working for Jermyn?"

"Provided you do as you're told, you'll always be looked after, but don't cross him."

"How long have you been working for him?" I enquired.

"Five years, and I'm still very happy."

"Were you always his driver?"

"No, I started out like you, but then moved to being his driver."

"So you were also hustling?"

"Yep!"

"And what about his clients; are there any really kinky ones?"

"Not really, but sometimes when he gets new ones, they can be a little bit of a problem, but his regulars are fine."

"And tell me, do you have to bring them to me or do I have to go to Jermyn's mansion? How does it work?"

"None will come to your place. There might be times when he'll call you to his mansion but in most cases you'll be taken to their houses or apartments."

"By the way, what's your name?"

"Gavin. I know that you're Chad. I watched the premiere of your movie and I think you're a prize catch."

"Thanks, Gavin. So tell me are you the only driver that he has or are there other guys who might pitch up to collect me?"

"There is one other guy by the name of Fernando, whose Spanish, but he works pert-time when I'm off or if we're really busy and need two drivers."

The pictures were being painted for me and I was beginning to realize that this was a well-organized business that Jermyn was running. It also interested me to know that if he was working only with up-market clients, then my income might improve.

"Gavin, are there any people I need to be wary of, either as clients or staff?"

"No, not really. Fernando could be a bit horny if he likes you, and you might find yourself being driven to some dark place where he might try to have some fun with you, but other than that, the regulars are not a problem."

I felt a lot more comfortable having spoken to Gavin about the ins and outs of the Jermyn enterprise. We finally reached my apartment block and I thanked Gavin for the drive, went upstairs, showered and then fell into my bed to dream of the future.

CHAPTER 18

MY FIRST CUSTOMERS

My first customers, and I emphasize the word 'customers', was a group of Jermyn's friends. He had decided to have what he affectionately called a 'welcoming party' for me and had invited a number of his male friends to come and view and 'taste' the new boy he had acquired.

I had been picked up from my apartment earlier in the afternoon by Gavin and taken back to the mansion where a set of clothes had been laid out for me in a private bedroom.

On the way to the mansion, Gavin had filled me in on what was expected to happen at the party and what I was expected to do or not do. I would be given a bedroom and it would be in there that the action would take place. Just so I didn't arrive looking like a street slut, new clothes would be laid out for me and before the evening's entertainment, I would be served a meal. After the evening's entertainment, Gavin would drive me home and hand me my earnings for the night. Apparently Jermyn never passed money on to his hustlers or 'boys' as he like to call us. One thing I will say about Jermyn, was that he always said he had the best boys available, and when I eventually got the opportunity once to meet all the other hustlers in Jermyn's employ, I realized that he was right.

Back at the mansion, I was led up to the bedroom allocated to me and saw the double bed and the new clothes lying on it. Everything was supplied. I had a white jockstrap, white jeans and a blue metallic-colored shirt to wear over my white jeans. White socks and shoes were also supplied. Naturally, once the evening's entertainment was over, I would change back into my everyday clothes and leave the new clothes at the mansion. I wondered if these clothes were shared among the boys at all.

After I'd eaten and showered, I pulled on my new jockstrap and admired myself in the mirror. I looked good. Then I pulled on the jeans and shirt and once again admired myself in the mirror. With the shirt on, I looked different. The sexiness seemed to have disappeared and I was worried that perhaps I might not be as attractive to Jermyn's guests as he had hoped I would, but I at least didn't choose the clothes, so I said nothing about it.

At approximately 8:00p.m, Jermyn's butler came to the room, knocked and entered.

"Jermyn is ready for you now," he said, ushering me downstairs to the lounge.

When I entered I was surprised to see so many people there. They were all shapes and sizes and amidst them I saw Jermyn sitting like royalty in a high-backed chair, holding court. People were fawning all over him and it wasn't until the butler caught his attention, did he rise and see me.

"Chad!" He shouted across the room. "Come here boy and meet my friends."

I strode confidently across the room to where he was now standing. When I reached him, I smiled and he took my hand.

"Gentlemen, this is my latest acquisition, Chad. If you haven't seen it yet, you must see my latest movie, *Jason and the Argonauts*. Chad is the star of that movie and he's got everything you want in a boy; the body, the equipment and he knows how to use it – I have already tested him."

The group of guests all laughed at Jermyn's comment and pretty soon I was being admired and prodded like it was a cattle market. My ass was patted and pinched; my biceps were felt and a couple even felt my crotch. My chest was rubbed and one man opened my shirt to take a look at my nipples, while another inspected my hands; why, I don't know. After everyone had taken a look at the new boy on the block, they returned to their drinks and chatting while I wandered around the room making small talk with whomever wanted to talk to me.

This continued until about 10:00p.m when Jermyn called me over to him.

"I think it's time you went up to your room, Chad. The first of your customers will be coming up to you. Be charming and don't let me down," said Jermyn smiling sweetly at me.

I made my way back to my room and waited. I wasn't sure whether I was expected to take my clothes off and wait, but hen I thought the customer might like doing it for me, so I remained dressed.

The first customer arrived. His name was Mel and he was Jewish. He looked about fifty-something and was short, but when he peeled off his clothes, I must say that he was well-hung, which suited me. Mel was only interested in a blow-job, which I delivered to perfection and sweet Mel left with a glow on his face and a spring in his step.

He was soon followed by a character called Little Joe. I take it you'll understand why he was called that name by his friends? He removed his pants and stood in front of me waiting for his blow-job, but there wasn't much to 'blow'. I did my best with what I was offered, but Little Joe seemed pleased with what I did for him, so he left with a smile on his face. So far the customers seemed to be pleased and only required a simple blow-job.

The evening progressed and a few more of Jermyn's friends came to test the new boy and left well- pleased. At about 1:00a.m I was told that Big Daddy wanted a taste of the new boy, so I awaited the man in my bedroom.

There was a polite knock on the bedroom door and I called out for the person to enter. A tall, muscular African-American walked in, oozing charm. His shaven head gleamed in the bright light of the bedroom and his biceps bulged as they tried to escape the confines of the T-shirt he was wearing. His jeans clung tightly to his tree-trunk legs and I noticed with awe, the size of the package that came with the jeans.

My mind went into turmoil when I saw the size of the package he was carrying, and panic set in. All evening I'd coped well with the blow-jobs, but I envisioned what he had hidden in his jeans might be a mouthful!

He walked over to the bed, kicked off his shoes and lay down, with a contented smile on his face.

"Come boy, do you want this?" He asked holding his crotch.

I moved over to the bed and looked down at the huge man. My groin was sweating with excitement and I just wanted to rip off his clothes, but wasn't sure exactly what he wanted.

I unbuttoned his jeans and moved to the bottom of the bed where I took the legs of his jeans and pulled, pulling them off of him. His Calvin Klein's bulged where his massive cock and balls lay, waiting to be pampered. Once his jeans were off, I crept up the bed between his thick thighs until I reached the massive package. My tongue began to salivate over the cotton material as I tasted his meat and I worked my way between his legs. I then moved up to the waistband of his briefs and saw how his swelling cock was beginning to escape the confines of his briefs. I licked the brown, cut head with my tongue and tasted some of his juice oozing from the tip. Taking hold of the waist band, I began to pull his briefs down to his ankles. What bounced at me can only be described as extraordinary. He had such a fine, thick cock that bent slightly to the left. Although his shaft was thick, he had one of those beautifully bulbous cock heads that seem to spread your chute as it sinks into you. Oh yes, this is what I wanted and I knew he wanted my ass to treat his mighty cock well.

There and then, I leapt from the bed, ripped off my clothes and grabbing a condom and some lube, jumped back onto the bed and prepared Big Daddy for my onslaught. As I rolled the condom down his long, thick shaft, I admired his manhood with a sense of loving care. To me it was like a fragile object that needed to be handled with care. Slowly the sheer rubber rolled down until it came to a halt and still a quarter of Big Daddy's cock was unsheathed. I inserted my fingers into my warm chute and readied myself, then I slowly lowered my ass onto his waiting weapon.

I felt him stretching my chute as he sank into me with an upward thrust. Fortunately he was gentle and there was no punishing pain as he entered me. I felt my head spinning as he went deeper and as I held my breath, so I went further and further until I was completely impaled on his cock, and then I sighed and breathed out.

"Just hold it there, Big Daddy, so I can get used to you."

He grinned at me.

"I'm proud of you boy. You're one of the few guys who can take me all the way and make me feel horny when I'm inside of you. I just want to fuck that tight ass of yours," he said, placing his hands on my ass cheeks and spreading them wider.

Once he sensed I was comfortable with his size, he started thrusting upwards and impaling me with deep, long thrusts that tickled my prostate and sent my eyes rolling in my head.

I have never shot my load so quickly and without touching myself, but it wasn't to end there. He continued pounding my ass until I came a second time and he shot his wad into me, then as gently as he'd entered me, so he gently withdrew and pulled me to his chest and kissed my forehead. The whole experience was one of awe and something I've seldom experienced from a man.

Once we were both dressed, Big Daddy hugged me to his massive chest and said he see me again, which pleased me; then he left the room.

At three in the morning, Gavin drove my tired body back to my apartment and handed me an envelope once we reached my home. I thanked Gavin for the lift and once inside, I opened the envelope and out fell $500 along with a small note saying how pleased Jermyn was with the comments his friends had made.

This was my beginning of things to come.

After a time, I got to know the likes and dislikes of Mel, Little Joe, Big Fat Oswald, Big Daddy and his horse-hung cock which plowed my ass regularly, Slim, and of course, Jermyn. Sometimes they took turns fucking my ass, one after the other, but on other occasions, Big Daddy would plow into my ass with his long cock, while the others stood around stroking their cocks until they shot their loads over me. This was one of the group's favorite pastimes and I enjoyed their enthusiasm, but of all Jermyn's friends, I had a passion for Big Daddy because of the way he used his cock to drive me crazy with desire.

One evening, Jermyn sent Gavin to collect me and along with Jermyn, they took me to the home of a client who had made a booking. The client, it turned out, was a friend of a friend of Jermyn's and who liked to be fucked but didn't advertise the fact to the world, as he portrayed himself as a bit of a he-man.

We arrived at the house and although Jermyn accompanied me indoors, he didn't sit in the bedroom and watch. I must admit, I had become used to performing in front of others as this had been the custom in Jermyn's house, so it wouldn't have worried me if Jermyn had decided to watch.

There was one outstanding feature about the client – he was a midget.

Now I have nothing against small people no matter what size they are, but this particular client liked to be carried around the room while being fucked, but it didn't end there; he had a dildo which he insisted had to be inserted into him along with the hustler's cock. I was beginning to find my kinky clients.

We both undressed and I was surprised because I thought that being a midget, his cock might be small, but it wasn't.

"Lie on the bed," said the midget, his voice matching his height, short and sharp!

I wanted to laugh when he squeaked out the instruction but I did as I was instructed and then he leapt onto the bed and began sucking my cock to get it hard. His frantic slurping sounds added to the humor and I was finding it difficult to get an erection, but once he felt my cock was hard enough, he stood stride me and lowered himself onto my shaft, sinking his ass onto it until he rested on my stomach. He had a serious look on his face, but then he took hold of his dildo and slowly slid it in alongside of my cock.

His face suddenly changed to one of joy and pleasure.

For me it was great to feel something rub along my shaft and in fact it brought with it a sense of complete satisfaction. Once he had embedded the dildo in his ass, he instructed me to lift him while he wrapped his legs around my waist. I did as he requested and then I was told to stand. I stood up with the little man impaled on my hard cock, and then with one hand he began thrusting the dildo in and out of his ass so that it gave both him and me pleasure while I carried him around the bedroom. I must be honest, it brought an intense feeling to me and I was very happy to fuck that ass of his until we both shot our loads and he pulled out the dildo which was covered with my warm cum. After Jermyn and I left the midget's house, I was asked what I had thought of the man. Not wanting to offend the friend of the friend, I said he was a good fuck, thereby avoiding saying anything about the person as such, however, I was tempted to say how funny I had found the entire episode.

"Why?" I asked.

"Because he'd like to see you again," replied Jermyn. "You obviously made a good impression on him."

This is what often happened to me; I wouldn't take something seriously and then it would backfire on me. The midget was the last person I would have gone out of my way to see, but because I did my job properly, he wanted me back. Now I would have to go through the same things again and still not laugh.

CHAPTER 19

THE KINKY CUSTOMERS

By no means can I tell you about all the kinky customers that I had to endure, but some stick out in my mind.

While working for Jermyn, I had no fixed hours but I had to be available 24 hours a day. This meant that sometimes I might be called at 9:00 or 10:00 in the morning to satisfy some client, or it might be midnight that some drunken person wanted to try to get a hard-on in order to screw me.

I preferred the night trade, because it usually included a wider variety of guys, but having said that, they also included the weird, who wanted to be burnt or tied up and beaten, which I found difficult to do.

I remember one early evening a woman approached Jermyn and said that she wanted me to go with her so that I could fuck her husband while she watched. It sounded a bit kinky at first, but then money is money.

I made it clear to Jermyn that I wasn't interested in the woman and that the arrangement was between me and the husband. I had no objections to her watching, but there was to be no participation with her or I would walk away from the deal. Fortunately Jermyn respected my wishes and also knew my likes and dislikes; not that I disliked women, but I wasn't into having sex with them.

When we arrived at the house, that is Gavin the driver and me, the wife was there to meet me. She led me into their lounge and there was the husband. He actually turned out to be quite good looking with a good body, but the wife was not too hot. I had made it plain to her that she was not to participate and that it was me and the husband; what she did while she watched was her business.

They had a pretty up-market house and I could see from the interior that money was not an issue. I was introduced to the husband who knew what was going to happen and didn't seem perturbed by it, so I thought that this might be a regular occurrence with them.

We then went into their bedroom and the husband stripped and so did I, while the wife sat in an easy chair admiring the two naked men.

"Now fuck him!" ordered the wife.

I lay the guy on his back on the bed and lifted his legs to spread his ass. His pucker winked at me as he anticipated my entry. I pushed forward and watched as my bulbous cock head sank slowly between the tight lips until my cock had begun to disappear into his chute. Both of us gasped as I sank deeper into him and felt the tight constriction around my shaft, and then I started pushing and pulling my shaft in and out of his ass while the wife began fingering herself in the easy chair. I decided not to watch her and focus on the husband, after all I could sense that he was enjoying himself with me and I certainly was getting some helluva pleasure from his tight ass.

Because of the tightness of his ass, it didn't take me long to come and as I did, I stroked his cock and brought him to his climax. I didn't really take much notice of the wife but I found the situation interesting, however, I never saw either again.

On another occasion, Jermyn sent me to the house of two gay men who were both into leather. Now I must admit that I find leather sexy; the smell of the material and the soft touch on the body does things to me that no other material does – maybe with the exception of Lycra.

Gavin had been given instructions to drive me to their house and to wait for me until they were finished. We drove for about half an hour until we reached the outskirts of town, where we came across a ranch-style house. I thought it rather quaint and Gavin and I had discussed the couple on the way there. He had told me that they had used guys from Jermyn before and although some of the guys had complained about their treatment, Jermyn had not banned them from requesting his boys. Was Gavin giving me a warning about these two men? Or was it that the other guys couldn't handle the treatment that the men dished out?

As we got out of the car, the front door to the house opened and out stepped two men. They were both in the region of six feet something in height and both were encased in leather: leather jeans, leather boots, leather harnesses, one had on a leather jockstrap and chaps, and leather waistcoats over their harnesses. I could immediately feel a reaction between my legs.

"Are you going to stay in the car, Gavin?"

"Well, I don't suppose I'm allowed to come in."

"Personally, I think I'd be happier if you were near me," I said, quietly so the two men never heard.

"Hi!" came a chorus from the steps to the front door.

"Hi!" I shouted back. "Any objections if my driver comes in as well?" I asked beaming a friendly smile at them.

They looked Gavin over, then mumbled something between them and finally allowed Gavin to come in rather that sitting in the car outside while he waited.

As we entered their house, I couldn't resist looking at their tightly encased asses. The leather covering their ass cheeks was smooth and tight, so much so, that I wanted to get on my knees there and then and start licking the smooth material.

Usually in these sorts of situations, the clients very seldom, if ever, offer you anything to drink, but tonight it was different. Both Gavin and I were offered a beer each, which we gladly accepted. We sat for a while drinking our beers and 'getting to know one another'.

Finally when the beers were finished, the slightly taller of the two, whose name was Kelly, suggested we go down into the basement. So Kelly, Joe, the other guy and I went downstairs while Gavin remained sitting in the lounge.

Down in the cellar basement, they had an Aladdin's cave of equipment, ranging from whips, paddles and cat-o-nine-tails to ropes, which I assumed were there for bondage – well at least I hoped that's what it was for, and dildos. It was quite a collection of contraptions. In the middle of the room hung a sling with chains attached to the ceiling. The two men started off by stripping me down to my briefs and when they saw I had on ordinary white briefs, they ripped them off and put me into a sleazy, stench-ridden jockstrap that probably belonged to one of them. I was then placed in the sling and my legs were hoisted up onto the chains to rest there, thereby exposing my ass to them. Kelly was the first to make a move. He tantalizingly dragged a finger across my ass hole a couple of times, causing my pucker to quiver, while Joe teasingly swung his jockstrap covered crotch in my face. I could see his sturdy legs encased in his chaps and to have his leather bound jockstrap in my face where I could smell the leather and taste its softness was enough to drive me crazy. While I was concentrating on Joe's bulging jockstrap, I had realized that Kelly had lubed up my ass and was busy inserting a black, fat dildo into me. I could feel my asshole stretch as the dildo slid in and as I gasped, so Joe thrust his crotch into my mouth.

Joe stood above my head while my mouth and tongue lathered his leather jockstrap and at the same time, I felt an excruciating pain: Joe had clamped two crocodile clamps onto my tender nipples. Again I gasped and again his crotch was thrust into my mouth. Kelly, in the meantime was pushing his dildo further into my ass and then pulling it out. This continued for sometime and then I felt it escape me, only to be replaced by Kelly's hand. I felt his fingers slide in and then spread to open my ass up. Gradually, he slid his while hand into my opening. I cried out with pain, but he ignored it. At the same time, Joe had removed his jockstrap and his long uncut cock was displayed to me and he swung it across my mouth, encouraging me to open my mouth and take his length into my throat. I managed to grab his cock, hold it still and insert it into my throat. As I sucked, so Kelly sank his wrist and hand deeper into my ass. Thank goodness I had taught myself to relax so, although it felt uncomfortable, the pain was not as I had expected. However, I slowly felt his arm begin to slide out of me and as it escaped, I breathed a sigh of relief.

"Time to changes, Joe," said Kelly, moving to the head of the swing. "His ass is ready for you."

Joe moved to between my legs and, aiming his long cock at my pulsating opening, he sank his dick into me until his balls slapped against my ass. As he held onto my hips and began fucking my ass, Kelly had lit a candle and was in the process of dripping wax onto my nipples, which by now had become accustomed to the tightness of the clamps. The hot wax startled my body each time it dropped onto my skin and when I felt the drips of wax begin to fall on my hard cock, it throbbed with each drop.

When Joe became tired of plowing into my ass, they swapped places again, but this time as Kelly sank his thick cock into my well-worn ass, he slapped my ass cheeks with a leather paddle he'd picked up. Between the two men, they spread my ass with whatever they could lay their hands on and finally after they had both shot their load onto my stomach and chest, they proceeded to piss on me. That was like the final dénouement; the final act of their pleasure.

They helped me to get out of the sling and with their piss dripping off me they escorted me to a shower in the basement where they both cleaned me, their rough hands running over my skin as though they were trying to get rid of the evidence. Once I was clean and dry, the two men thanked me for my participation and we went back upstairs. Gavin was still waiting in the lounge and after they had handed Gavin the required fee, we left for my apartment.

"Are you OK?" asked Gavin, tenderly.

For a moment I was still, not saying a word as I tried to take everything in. Then I caught his eye in the car's rear view mirror and I tried to smile to say that I was OK.

My ass was as tender as anything from the pummeling I had received and I felt dirty, even though they had showered and cleaned me. Is this really what I wanted in life?

When we arrived at my apartment, Gavin stopped the car and switched off the engine. He got out of the driver's seat, came round to my side, opened the car door and helped me out. He walked with me into the foyer of the building and then came up in the elevator with me. I was walking like an old man. Neither of us spoke until we reached my apartment door.

"Give me the keys, Chad."

I handed Gavin the keys and we entered. He helped me to the couch and gently sat down.

"Chad, can I get you anything to drink?"

"Something strong, please Gavin. You'll find the drinks in the kitchen and help yourself to something."

As Gavin went in search of drinks for us, I closed my eyes and visions of the evening flashed before me. My ass felt tender and my legs, from being hoisted all that time, felt drained and tired.

Gavin returned with a scotch for me and a beer for himself, and then he sat in a chair opposite me.

"Are you sure you're OK? You look as if you're in pain."

I tried to smile, but even that seemed painful.

"It's my ass, Gavin. I think they've split me open."

"What did they do to you?" asked Gavin, feeling for his fellow worker.

"The fucking was nothing; it was when Kelly fisted me. I've never had that before and I'm sure he split me wide open when he sank his arm into me. Do you know what I feel like?"

"What?"

"A bath. Would you mind very much running some water for me so that I can just soak in it?"

Gavin ran to the bathroom and rapidly filled the bath with warm water and then helped me to undress and get into the bath.

"You don't have to leave," I said as Gavin was about to walk out of the bathroom. "I'll probably need you to help me get out of here when I'm finished."

Gavin sat on the side of the bath and watched me lying there soaking. I noticed how he very seldom took his eyes off my cock as it floated and bobbed in the warm water.

"You sure as hell have been blessed, Chad, you've got one of the biggest dicks I've ever seen."

I gave a slight smile. I felt drawn closer to Gavin through his kindness and concern.

Once I had soaked for about half an hour, Gavin helped me out of the bath and dried me, and then he helped me to my bed, pulled down the sheets and laid me in the bed.

"Now that I know you're safe and secure, I'll leave you. I've left your money in the envelope in the lounge. You can get it in the morning."

"Thanks Gavin, I really appreciate you being here for me tonight. Listen, it's late so if you want to stay the night, you're welcome to."

"I'd love to Chad, but I have to get the car back to the boss, you know."

Gavin gave me a gentle kiss on the check, switched off the bedroom light, said, "I'll call you in the morning to see how you are, but I'll also tell Jermyn that you're in no state to work for a couple of days."

With that, he left and very soon tiredness and sleep overtook me.

CHAPTER 20

THE PARTY

Out of my incident with Kelly and Joe, a number of things emerged; I remembered the words of Gavin when I questioned him about Jermyn and how he ran his business. Gavin had said 'Provided you do as you're told, you'll always be looked after.' He was right because when Gavin informed Jermyn how I was and he thought I'd be out of action for a while, Jermyn contacted me to find out how I was. However, it didn't end there; because it amazed me how many of my regulars were also told about me being out of action for a while. Big Daddy called me to ask if he could do anything for me, including "do you want me to fuck those guys up?" I was genuinely flattered to think that all these guys really considered me as part of their 'family' and that I must have been doing something right to earn their respect and admiration.

So often hustlers are seen only as a form of escapism for guys with over-enthusiastic hormones and are there for other's convenience, but I was surprised to see how Jermyn and his close friends rallied round to support me. I know it might sound melodramatic, me being laid up for a while, but I'd never been fisted in my life and it wasn't done in a way that a novice might be introduced to the experience. My ass was genuinely painful and the last thing I wanted or needed was someone wanting to book me and then screw me, especially Big Daddy.

"I promise I'll make it up to you when I'm able," I had told Big Daddy when he had contacted me to find out how I was.

"You just take it easy and get that cute, tight ass of yours back in working order and let me know when you're ready," he had said.

While this was happening, I was nearing my twenty-first birthday and my Mum and Dad had asked if I wanted a party to celebrate. I liked the idea, but I realized that this might be awkward, considering that all my friends were guys and many were in the 'entertainment' industry, which I didn't think my folks would appreciate.

"But why don't you want a party, son?" enquired my mother, on the phone.

I couldn't tell her of my life-style, so instead I suggested they save their money and just have an intimate dinner at their place. Obviously she'd planned to invite all their friends and I was now putting a spanner in the works, but with some gentle persuasion, she relented and it was decided that I'd go round for dinner on my birthday.

However, unbeknown to me, Jermyn was planning a party at his mansion in honor of my twenty-first birthday. Fortunately I'd mentioned the dinner with my parents, so the two events wouldn't clash.

I won't bore you with details of the dinner party, but Jermyn's party for me was a bash to end all bashes. All his current boys were invited as well as some of the guys I'd worked with at *Virilis Films*, including Marc and Josh, and health-wise, I was back to normal.

Gavin had picked me up in the Cadillac on the night of the party and driven me to the mansion where cars were cluttering up the grounds. Inside, the lounge had been stripped of most of its furniture to make room for the guests and Jermyn had given me a room for the night as a treat, so I could enjoy myself and not have to worry about leaving to get home. I wondered, however, if there was a catch to the treat, and I was right; Jermyn did spend some of the night in my bed.

As I entered the house on the night of the party, everyone burst into song and, situated on a large round table in the middle of the lounge, were literally piles of brightly wrapped presents. Part of the fun of the evening was when Jermyn insisted that I open some of the presents. Obviously he'd arranged with some of his friends to make it a fun evening, because when I opened the presents, we were all in fits of laughter. Among the exciting gifts I received were: two satin G-strings, three different sized dildos, a beautifully designed cock ring in silver, a studded leather jockstrap, a voucher for a massage at a local male massage parlor and a basket filled with lubes, flavored condoms and a mystery invitation to spend the night with the person who gave it to me. Unfortunately there was no name on the basket to say who it was from – the idea was for me to try and find out.

"What happens if I don't find out who gave me this present?" I asked, referring to the hamper of goodies.

"Then the person will phone you tomorrow," replied Jermyn.

He obviously knew who the person was, but was not divulging.

A sumptuous supply of food was on offer and drinks flowed freely. I don't know how much this must have cost Jermyn, but I really appreciated both his kindness and the way the people rallied around to support him in preparing the party.

The music blared forth and everyone danced the night away. Naturally, a party like this when you have so many hustlers in one place and so many eager clients, can only lead to fun and games. Jermyn had decided that for once, should it happen, if a client fancied a little something with one of his hustlers, if was free, provided it took place within the bounds of the property.

By midnight, the numbers in the lounge had diminished slightly and bodies could be seen lurking among the foliage of the grounds. All the bedrooms had been declared 'out of bounds', but any other room could be used, so bathrooms and even the kitchen became a hive of activity. As the center of attraction, being my party, I decided to try and remain as celibate for the night as possible, but I must admit, it was extremely hard. You've got to understand that when you're surrounded by close to a hundred good looking men and some not so good looking, but well-endowed, it becomes problematic to keep your clothes on. Hands cupped my ass at times while others stroked my arms and chest and one or two even groped my crotch, but throughout, I tried to keep my cool.

At one rare stage I was standing alone at the drinks table when Marc appeared and took me by the hand. He led me out through the French door into the garden and walked me to a spot well hidden from the bright lights of the lounge. He planted a kiss on my lips, his tongue forcing entry into my mouth. I immediately felt myself become aroused, but at the same time, I could feel his arousal pressing against me, then I felt his hand slide down to my crotch and squeeze my cock.

With our lips locked, he fumbled with my zipper and finally hauled my hard cock out into the cool night air. It wasn't out for very long because he left my lips and sank to his knees where he wrapped his warm mouth around my shaft and began sucking my length.

After a while, he stopped and looked up at me in the dark.

"You always do this for others, now it's your turn," he said before resuming his erotic actions.

I could feel myself getting closer and closer to shooting, so I warned Marc, but that didn't deter him. He increased his speed, taking my cock deeper into his throat until I couldn't hold on any longer and with a loud groan, fired my load down his throat. Marc was good. He never let a single drop of seed escape his throat and he continued sucking until he felt my cock was dry of any more liquid, and then he rose to his feet and again locked his lips to mine. I could taste my seed in his mouth as our tongues dueled together. We kissed long and tenderly.

"What about you?" I asked, wanting to know whether he wanted to come.

"I have already," replied Marc.

"When?"

"Now. While I was sucking you off, I shot my bolt," he said coyly.

"Oh wow! Was it that good for you?"

He smiled and nodded, and then holding hands, we returned to the lounge, looking flushed. Those who saw us knew that we'd had a good time.

As I have already said, I had the use of a bedroom at Jermyn's mansion for the night, and so when all the guests started to drift off, either to other parties or to go home, I made my way up to my room with Jermyn. When we entered the room, he picked me up and carried me to the bed, almost like a bridal couple.

"What's that for?" I questioned.

"I just felt like doing it," he replied.

He laid me gently on the bed and sank down next to me.

"I hope you've had a wonderful party tonight, Chad."

"I have, I have, and thank you so much for all you've done for me. I really do appreciate it. In fact I can't thank you enough, Jermyn."

We slowly undressed each other and once we were naked, I turned to him and asked, "What would you like tonight?"

"Just to sleep with you, to hold you, kiss you and maybe make love to you."

The fact that he'd said 'make love' made me think that perhaps it wasn't going to be one of his rushed jobs where there was no finesse or passion and simply a lustful fuck.

I was right. He was gentle and caring tonight and I enjoyed it when he buried his hard cock inside of me. I treated him like a king and gave him whatever he wanted; it was my only way of saying 'thank you' for the party.

The following morning, Gavin was there to drive me home to my simple apartment. All the way home, I sat in the car as though I was on cloud nine, reminiscing the night before and all the wonderful people who'd been there to celebrate with me.

When I arrived home, my dad was waiting at the entrance to the building for me. He saw the smart car and the 'chauffeur' and asked whose it was. Now I had a problem.

"Let's go upstairs, Dad."

"Would you like some tea or coffee?" I asked when we entered my apartment.

"Whose car was that, son?"

"I was given a surprise birthday party by the financier to the film company and it's his car."

"Have you been partying all night then?"

"No, I stayed there last night, and that's why his driver's just brought me home now."

I saw the look on my Dad's face and was wondering what his next question was going to be; but it never came. He remained silent.

"Coffee will be fine, son."

I went into the kitchen to make the coffee and when I came out, I saw my dad standing by the window, looking out.

"Chad, can I ask you something?"

Oh boy, here it comes, I thought.

"Sure Dad."

"Those boys who work downstairs; the ones that you're friendly with, do you do what they do?"

I went cold. I'm sure my face must have gone white with shock. He never looked at me as he said it, but he waited for my answer. I went over to the window and stood next to him.

"I have done, Dad."

"To make ends meet, no doubt?"

"Yes Dad. It's just that I didn't want to ask you for money when I was down and out."

Silence.

"Do you still do it?"

"Not down on the street, Dad."

He turned and looked at me.

"What do you mean 'not down on the street'? Does that mean you do it, but some other way?"

I hung my head. I couldn't look into his face.

"Do you have a pimp, then?"

This was becoming more and more awkward.

"That man who gave you the party, is he your pimp?"

Silence.

"I presume your silence means, 'yes'?"

I managed to raise my head slightly and my eyes caught his sad look. I was convinced that I had now destroyed my dad's impression of me, that the only son he had, and whom he had looked up to as a budding film star, was nothing more than a common hustler, much like the thousand who frequented the streets of America.

He turned to me and embraced me in his arms, but tightly. Not a word was spoken and I could only grab onto him and hug him as though I knew he'd forgiven me. We stood like this for what seemed like ten minutes, with neither saying anything, and then he released his hold slightly and looked at me.

"You know I love you."

"Yes, Dad."

"And I have never stood in your way with anything."

"Yes, Dad."

"I just want you to know that no matter what you do with your life, I'll always love you, but I am asking you to please be careful."

"I am, Dad."

"When I say be careful, I don't only mean about condoms and things like that; I'm also talking about who you go with. Don't let anyone hurt you in any way, promise me that."

I knew it was difficult to promise that because sometimes you never knew the client and never knew what might be in store for you, but nevertheless, I promised. What surprised me was the concern in my Dad's voice for my well-being.

"Sit down, son. I want to tell you something."

We sat down next to each other on the couch, me holding his hand in mine.

"What we've discussed today stays in this apartment and neither your mother nor your grandmother will ever know. Agreed?"

"Agreed!" I replied.

"When I was your age, I went through much the same things you are going through. I was also down and out when I left home and to get some income, I did what you are doing."

I looked shocked by this revelation.

"You mean…!"

"Yes, I was also a hustler. That is until I'd made enough money to get myself on the straight and narrow and then I met your mother and things changed. That's why I am in no position to criticize what you are doing, but your mother never knew what I had done."

I didn't know how to respond, other than hug my Dad to me. Now things began to make sense. Maybe when I saw him give Hank some money it was because he'd been through all this and understood the hardship that the hustlers go through.

"But tell me about this pimp. What's his name and how does he treat you?"

I explained Jermyn to him and told my Dad that I didn't work the streets and that it was private and therefore I got more money than the street boys. Yes I had worked once with Hank, but it was safer and better to work for Jermyn because he looked after his boys and there was no drugs and we had to keep ourselves fit and in shape. I even went so far as to tell my Dad about the episode with Kelly and Joe and how all Jermyn's regulars had rallied around to see that I was OK. Once he heard that, he was happier that I was being cared for.

When we'd finished our coffee and my Dad was about to leave, I held him in, my arms once more, kissed him tenderly as a son might kiss his father and then posed the question that had been lurking in the back of my mind.

"Tell me Dad; were you a top or a bottom?" I asked with a cheeky grin.

"Always versatile, son, it brings in more money."

CHAPTER 21

A HAPPY RESOLUTION

A while after my meeting with my dad, I was sitting on a bench in the local park, just taking time out, when a guy of about thirty-something approached and sat down on the bench beside me. Out of the corner of my eye, I noticed how slick he was dressed and that he also had a handsome look about him. Neither of us spoke at first, but then after a couple of minutes, he started the conversation.

"Pretty pleasant here, isn't it?"

"Yes, it is," I replied, turning to have a good look at him.

He looked the sort who hung out at the gym and took care of his body. The chest could be seen stretching the thin cotton material of his shirt and through the tightness I could make out two plump nipples, extending to try and break free.

"Do you come here often?" asked the stranger.

"Not really, but it seemed such a nice day, I thought I'd come and take a break."

"A break from what?"

"Oh just a break," I continued, not wanting to say what I did.

I thought it odd that the stranger might be out here in the park on a working day. Why wasn't he in a suit and at work?

"Are you on holiday?" I asked.

"No, why?"

"Well, it's just that you usually see businessmen here during the day in their suits, and not guys in casuals."

"But you're casually dressed," he retorted.

"Sure, but that's my work clothes."

"So what do you do?"

I hesitated at first, but then relinquished.

"Let's just say I try to bring pleasure to others."

"Oh!" smiled the stranger. "You're a hustler then?"

I nodded embarrassedly.

"Nothing wrong with that," replied the stranger, taking a closer look at me. "One thing I'll say, you at least look good. So many look weather-beaten and worn out, but you look fresh and healthy."

"I try to stay fit," I answered.

"Does someone look after you?"

"If you mean do I have a pimp, yes."

"From the look on your face, I'd say you don't seem too happy with the guy."

"It's not that I'm unhappy with the guy, it's just that I have other thoughts on my mind."

"Have you got problems with the guy?"

"No. It's just that I'm thinking of giving it all up."

"But with your looks and good body, surely the money's good?"

"Sure it is, but it's not just that. I'd like to settle down."

The stranger extended a hand to me.

"Gary's the name," he said, "and I'm offering myself to you."

I looked stunned by his statement.

"I'm Chad, but how do you mean offering yourself to me?"

"I'd like to take you back to my place and if I like what I see and get, I'd like to take care of you and your business, if that's OK with you?"

I looked at Gary and wondered if it might not be a police trap, but then I agreed to go with him.

As we traveled in the cab to his apartment, he asked a variety of questions about me, my age, how long I'd been a hustler and so on. When we arrived at his apartment, I was stunned to see how beautifully it was furnished and laid out. He offered me something to drink and then we made our way to his bedroom and sank onto his plush double bed.

"I want to get one thing clear," he said, as he pulled off his shirt to reveal his buff, well-chiseled chest, "I want to fuck that ass of yours, but I also want you to fuck mine."

This sounded like a double treat as I enjoyed a good looking, muscular man, having my ass, when I wasn't fucking someone. I stripped off my shirt and then Gary undid my jeans, allowing then to drop to the floor.

"I like what I see," said Gary, when he saw I had no underwear on, except for a semi-hard cock.

I kicked off my shoes and helped him undress. The man was extremely well-hung and the moment I saw his hardening cock, all I wanted to do was get to my knees and lick those heavy balls and the heavy cock shaft. I think he could see the lust in my eyes.

"I can see what you want, Chad, and my cock's just waiting for you to make love to it. Take it right down that throat of yours and suck me dry."

I didn't need a second invitation, and immediately began doing what he had wanted. My mouth worked frantically along his thick shaft, tasting every inch he had to offer, and slurping his balls into my warm mouth and sucking gently on them. Every so often, I looked up at Gary's face and saw pleasure etched across it.

After a while I rose from my knees and moved Gary onto the bed where I raised his legs into the air and positioned my face between his legs and began a tongue journey towards his pucker. When I found it, I inhaled his muskiness and thrust my tongue into his puckered opening.

"Ah fuck, that feels good," he murmured, lifting his legs higher to allow me easier access.

As my tongue loosened him up, so I slipped a finger into his opening and let it sink slowly into his depths until only my knuckles were visible. Gary's breathing and moaning had become louder and more intense as my fingers searched his chute, teasing his prostate at the same time.

"Oh yes, Chad! Fuck me! Stick that dick of yours up me and fuck the shit out of me! Aargh Fuuuck!"

Gary was writhing with pleasure on my finger and I realized he was ready. I withdrew my finger and, holding my firm shaft and guiding it closer to his pulsating asshole, I slowly sank into his warm, tight chute. A wave of ecstasy overcame me as I went deeper into him and with it he groaned loudly and pushed back onto my cock. As I slide slowly in and out of him, I admired the satisfied expression on his face. There was never a sign of discomfort or pain and it felt as though we were conjoined. I leant forward and placed my lips on his and as our tongues found each other, so I continued to rub my cock head against his prostate, giving him the pleasure such a handsome man deserved.

I felt how his ass muscles tightened around my cock as though he wanted to strangle my shaft and clamp it there for life, and with this tightness, I could feel myself getting closer and closer to coming.

"Careful, Gary; you're getting me close to shooting," I said, slowing down my movement, but immediately I felt him tighten his squeeze on my cock.

"Oh shit! I'm gonna shoot!" I exclaimed, firing into the warm confines of Gary.

I grunted and groaned as each shot was fired and with it, my body shuddered until I could feel Gary drain the last drops of warm cum from my balls. As I slowly withdrew from him, our lips remained sealed until I felt my subsiding cock feel the coolness of the bedroom.

"I'm yours now," I whispered as our mouths parted.

Gary smiled back at me and rolled me onto the bed with my back facing him. I felt him insert a finger into my ass which was still quivering as the last drops of cum escaped the tip of my cock and my cock gave a few more throbs. His finger was coated with lube and sank easily into my tunnel. He maneuvered his finger around inside of me and then, having loosened me up sank his thick cock into my waiting ass.

As I felt the large mushroom-shaped head break through my sphincter, I felt a dizzy feeling and I thought I saw stars. His cock was larger than I had expected and it stretched its way along my tunnel until his balls lapped up against my smooth ass. He held his position for a moment, savoring the feeling and then he began his leisurely pummeling of my ass. I could feel that this was not a purely physical experience, but that he rode me with passion and care. He knew how to use his weapon and he knew how to satisfy a guy.

I tightened my ass muscles and thrust back onto his long shaft until I could feel his breathing increase and he readied himself to shoot. His cock dug deep into my and his balls slapped loudly against my ass as he fired his load. When we had exhausted ourselves, we dressed and I headed back home.

That evening, Hank came up to the apartment, looking a little worse for wear. He'd had some rough clients and was battered and bruised, but that wasn't stopping him from looking for tricks. A strange feeling crossed me; I missed the excitement of the street with Hank, and although I was making good money with Jermyn, it was the sense of excitement that I found lacking in my life, yet there was still the nagging feeling of wanting to go into a relationship and quit the hustling.

"I think I should spend a night or two with you boys on the street again," I had said.

"We miss you, Chad," said Hank, his bruised face looking painful.

That night I was downstairs with the boys, but I never told Jermyn what I was doing, when a client by the name of Tony appeared. He had driven past me a couple of times because I recognized the Cadillac driving past, and then on the third or fourth drive-by, he stopped. I wandered over to the driver's window and peered in. I liked what I saw and we negotiated a deal – for a simple blow-job; but then he said he wanted something more.

He was good looking, had a trim, fit body, unlike some of my larger customers, and he was well-equipped. I liked the way his long, thick, circumcised cock rubbed against my prostate and how he teased my ass by just entering my asshole and then pulling out: that drove me crazy with desire. The other thing that drew me to Tony, which I found out later, was that he was married, but his wife was completely unaware of his dalliances with me.

The apartment to which he took me, was his 'business' office, or so he told his wife. He actually lived out of town and often had to stay the night in town for business reasons, and this was his pad when he did this.

"Why don't you get out of this type of work, Chad?" asked Tony, when we'd finished making love.

"The money's good," I answered "and it gives me the opportunity to see you."

"But what about the other guys that want you?"

"Some are OK, but others … you take your life in your hands with them."

"Do they ever beat you up?" asked Tony, with concern in his voice.

"Sure. A couple of times I've been beaten up …"

"…beaten up or was it S&M?"

"Mostly S&M gone a bit too far," I replied.

"…and you enjoyed that?" Queried Tony.

I laughed slightly.

"Not really, but you have to please the customer."

"And do you have a pimp?"

"Yeah."

"And what's he like?"

"A big brute of a guy but he's very kind to me. In fact I usually do up-market clients and it's by phone. I don't normally do the streets. It's just that I missed the excitement of the streets that I'm here."

Tony pulled me closer to him so that our erections rubbed against each other and out lips met in the dark.

As the night moved into day, so I rose from the warmth and comfort of Tony's bed, dressed, picked up my payment that was lying alongside of the bed, kissed him gently on the forehead and crept out of his apartment.

As I wandered down the street, looking for a cab, my mind began to think about what I was doing with my life, my future and what was to become of me when I got older and maybe couldn't perform any more.

It was also about this time that Marc came to see me with an idea that he had, and one which I suppose I might have had at the back of my mind, but had never thought of considering it.

"Chad, I have to tell you something that's been bugging me ever since I first met you," said Marc.

"And what's that?"

He became a little coy but eventually managed to say what he wanted to.

"I've always found you attractive, and I've noticed that whenever I see you, I don't want you to leave. Chad, I think what I'm trying to say, is that I think I love you. There now I've said it."

I was dumbstruck at first until I began to think about Marc and realized that my feelings were very much like his.

"It's funny that you say that, because I have found that whenever I'm withy you, there seems to be a calming effect and I find peace with you. I also find myself thinking unconsciously about you for no real reason, other than I probably also miss being with you."

"So? Where does that put us?"

"Are you suggesting we go into a relationship?" I asked, actually hoping he would say 'yes'.

Marc smiled broadly at me and nodded his head, but hesitantly at first. I returned the smile and we fell into each other's arms and kissed passionately.

"I have one question n to ask. What's going to happen about or work?" I asked.

"Obviously I would prefer you not to be hustling because after all, I'd want you to myself."

"But then how would I feel if I knew you were filming and some guy was fucking you and I wasn't there to do it?"

"Then we have to build our relationship on trust."

"I don't have a problem with that, Marc, but in truth, I relay would like to give up hustling and settle down in a relationship with you"

"Maybe I can speak to Mr. Hamilton and see if he'll employ you in the company again, then we could work together," suggested Marc.

"Would you do that?"

"If it meant us being together, yes. Maybe I can also have it pout in my contract that any sex scenes can only be done between you and me and I won't do any with any other guys."

"I appreciate that, Marc, but don't be too hard on yourself. Maybe say that you're willing to let guys give you a blow-job or a wank, but any other sex must be between us," I recommended.

We both glowed as we held each other and dreamed of better times together.

However, I will always remember the boys in my life, the ones who flitted through making little impact and the ones who made a mark on me, just as I will always remember some of my 'tricks' and what they taught me about life and being a hustler. I am glad that Marc came into my life and equally glad that he appeared that night to 'proposition' me.

Yes, there are times when I miss the company of Jermyn and I know I can still look out of my window and watch Hank and the boys below on the street, but I know I have something better; a beautiful man in my life and the knowledge that if I need to hustle, the only person who'll be my 'trick' is Marc.

ABOUT THE AUTHOR

Lew Bull

LEW BULL recently had his fifth novel published, entitled *Shadows*. This novel adds to his collection of mystery stories titled, *Power Buddies; Wet, Wild & Willing; The Bonds of Friendship* and *Caribbean Cruising*. Added to these are his recently published two anthologies, one of exotic cocktail recipes accompanied by equally erotic stories entitled, *Cocktales* and the other, *Mystique*. His novel *Wet, Wild & Willing* was nominated for the 2008 National Leather Association (International) writing award. Other recent anthologies that contain his work include, *Cruise Lines; Taken By Force; Boys Will Be Boys; Don't Ask, Don't Tie Me Up - Military BDSM Fantasies; Service with a Smile; Pretty Boys & Roughnecks; Special Forces* and *Sex Time-Travel*. He is still involved in education and lives in Johannesburg, South Africa where he enjoys spending time with his partner of thirty-two years and traveling as often as he can.

Power Buddies

a novel by
LEW BULL

A NOVEL BY
Lew Bull

WET, WILD AND WILLING

Bull

Wet, Wild
and Willing
The sexcapades of a single man

A
BONER
BOOK

SHADOWS

A NOVEL BY
LEW BULL

A
BONER
BOOK

tales

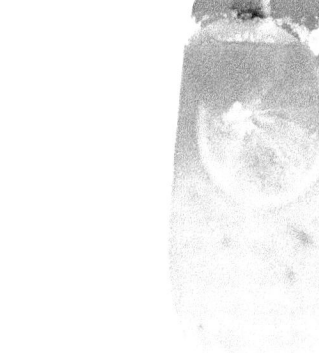

by

Lew Bull

Bull

Cocktales

Bull

The Bonds of
Friendship

a novel by

Lew Bull

A
Boner
Book

Caribbean Cruising

a novel by
Lew Bull

Bull

A Boner Book

BULL

MYSTIQUE

MYSTIQUE

LEW
BULL

A
BONER
BOOK

www.ingramcontent.com/pod-product-compliance
Lightning Source LLC
Chambersburg PA
CBHW051655260626
47170CB00004B/1513